POSSESSION

DIARY OF A HAUNTING

POSSESSION

M. VERANO

SIMON PULSE

NEW YORK   LONDON   TORONTO   SYDNEY   NEW DELHI

SIMON PULSE

An imprint of Simon & Schuster Children's Publishing Division

1230 Avenue of the Americas, New York, New York 10020

First Simon Pulse hardcover edition August 2016

Text copyright © 2016 by Simon & Schuster, Inc.

Jacket photographs copyright © 2016 by Kate Love/Arcangel Images (hands) and copyright © 2016 by Michael Frost (girl)

Interior images on pages 11, 35, 43, 48, 66, 78, 80, 91, 106, 165, 170, 195, 200, 203, 214, 233, 250, 255, 303, 305, 316, and 341 copyright © 2016 by Thinkstock

Interior images on pages 57, 101, 113, 117, 141, 155, 166, 176, 185, 189, 212, 219, 238, 281, and 315 copyright © 2016 by Amy Danziger Ross

SIMON PULSE and colophon are registered trademarks of Simon & Schuster, Inc.

For information about special discounts for bulk purchases, please contact Simon & Schuster Special Sales at 1-866-506-1949 or business@simonandschuster.com.

The Simon & Schuster Speakers Bureau can bring authors to your live event. For more information or to book an event, contact the Simon & Schuster Speakers Bureau at 1-866-248-3049 or visit our website at www.simonspeakers.com.

Designed by Regina Flath

The text of this book was set in Berling Std.

Manufactured in the United States of America

2 4 6 8 10 9 7 5 3 1

This title has been cataloged with the Library of Congress.

ISBN 978-1-4814-6441-3 (hc)

ISBN 978-1-4814-6443-7 (eBook)

EDITOR'S NOTE

It is with a bitter mixture of scholarly excitement and deep personal sadness that I present this account of the strange events leading up to the tragic end of one young woman's life. Readers familiar with my earlier volume, *Diary of a Haunting*, will know of my commitment to the search for evidence of paranormal phenomena—some might even call it my obsession. The story that follows is the most startling documentation of the effects of supernatural forces I have ever yet encountered, and its significance to human understanding cannot be overestimated. It pains me, however, that this revelation comes at such a heavy cost.

The author of this text, called Laetitia here, is a singularly brave soul who endured unthinkable torments before developing a hard-won understanding of the forces afflicting her. In the eight months prior to the events reported here, she maintained an unremarkable Internet journal detailing her pursuit of a career as a musician and offering personal grooming tutorials to her followers. In January of 2014 the tone and content of her entries shifted as Laetitia became troubled by inexplicable physical symptoms. She began posting more locked entries that could not be viewed by her followers, and gradually started to use the blog more as a personal diary.

Upon Laetitia's death, her mother found the password for her blog among her things and read the private entries. Her mother was advised by a friend familiar with my previous work to pass the document on to me, and so I came into possession of this unique document. The horror I experienced in reading of Laetitia's bizarre condition is matched only by a determination to make such knowledge public, and thus serve both science and the memory of this remarkable young woman.

The journal has been lightly edited, mostly to protect Laetitia and her family's privacy, and to remove irrelevant passages that have no bearing on the tragic events that led to her death.

I can only hope Laetitia's family is comforted to know her courageous sacrifice has increased public understanding of the terrifying yet awe-inspiring anomalies that may be found on the fringes of human experience.

Montague Verano, Phd.
Professor, Department of History
University of Idaho

All identifying names, places, and images have been changed or removed to protect the anonymity of those involved.

MONDAY, JANUARY 6, 4:15 P.M. (PUBLIC)

Thank you all for your comments on my last tutorial on creating a two-tone wig! I'm glad it was useful. And you know, you can use that same technique to create more than two tones if you want to do three tones or go crazy and do, like, a million different colors. Actually, that would be difficult—you probably want to limit yourself to four or five at most.

And thanks to everyone who said I looked fabulous! You guys are the best.

(@⁺‿⁺@) <-- *blushing*

Sometimes people at school or on the street try to judge me for having pink or purple or turquoise hair, or wearing glittery eyelashes in the middle of the afternoon, but screw them.

You guys understand me and always know how to lift my spirits.

Speaking of which, today was rough. I lost my voice! Totally and completely lost it—I opened my mouth, and nothing at all came out. I panicked, of course. That's never happened to me before. . . . I've had sore or scratchy throats, and I've gotten hoarse, but never anything like this. Completely out of the blue. I can talk a little if I force it—croak like a frog, really. But what good does croaking do me when I'm supposed to be rehearsing every day? The open auditions for *America Sings* are only a few months away, and I definitely can't sing like this.

It's really stressing me out. I *have* to make that audition! When am I ever going to get another chance like this? A chance to sing in front of real TV producers from Hollywood? I need this. I know if they can just hear me, they will love me. But I *need* to be at that audition.

I've been working at this for so long. My whole life, really. And I can practice and post videos online and do all the little church solos I want, but none of that is going to make me a star. It's not enough to sing just for the people here, in my neighborhood, or the handful of people reading my blog. I want the whole world to hear my voice. And for the longest time, I didn't see how I was going to make that happen. No matter how bad you want something, you can't just will it into existence.

But with these auditions coming up, I feel like I finally have a chance. I'm not worried about my voice or my talent. . . . Mostly I'm worried about getting up there and freezing, and blowing my only shot at being famous. That's why I've been rehearsing so much.

I got permission to use the school auditorium when no one else is, and I go in there and stand in front of all those empty seats and force myself to imagine those bigwigs from Hollywood judging me and making me feel small and insignificant. And I focus all my energy on showing them I am *not* small or insignificant—in letting them see the real ~**laetitia**~. The one who has a date with destiny.

But I can't do it without my voice! That's kind of an important part of being a singer.

I've never experienced anything like this before, even in a nightmare. Gramma Patty says it's just a cold, nothing to worry about, and I want to believe her, but I've got to admit I'm a little nervous. My head keeps filling with all these horrible things it could be—polyps, cancer—but Gramma Patty made me gargle with salt water when I got home (blech), and now I have some hot tea with honey, and it does seem to be helping a bit. I'm going to get some rest, and hopefully, it will all be better in the morning.

In the meantime, I would really appreciate any thoughts and prayers you can send my way. This is *so* important to me, and I can use all the support I can get. Thank you!!! I love you all so much.

(/◐ヮ◐)/*:·°✧

Thank you for all the get-well-soon notes! I checked my messages this morning, and I was overwhelmed! You guys are the greatest.

I'm happy to say my voice is much better. There were one or two creaky moments when I was rehearsing after school, but nothing like yesterday. Hallelujah.

° · ✿ ˇ\(｡ ●‿●｡)/✿ · °

I was so happy I could talk and sing again, I decided to do an extraspecial ~*divanation*~ to celebrate. A pink-and-lavender wig with sparkly barrettes! Hope you like.

[photo redacted]

[photo redacted]

Since I got some new followers recently, I should explain: *divanation* is a word my best friend, Angela, made up when we were eleven, I think. It means "the process of making myself up like a diva." Turning plain old Laetitia into ~**laetitia**~, the fabulous diva who's going to rule the world with the power of her voice. I know it's silly, but it helps me be bold and confident to have this persona I put on every day. And it makes people treat me differently too. Back when I would go to school, looking ordinary, that's how everyone treated me. When I told them I was going to be a famous singer someday, they'd laugh or give me pitying looks. But when I put in a little effort every morning to look ~fabulous~, suddenly my dreams don't seem so crazy anymore. Now all my friends and teachers and everyone look at me like they see the person I am on the inside. Like they believe I'm capable of anything. And that helps, especially on days when I'm not so sure of it myself.

MONDAY, JANUARY 13, 4:17 P.M. (PUBLIC)

It happened again! My voice disappeared. Now I am seriously worried. (✿☉_☉)

Last time, I woke up the next morning and felt 1,000 percent better, and I was *so* relieved. I could talk again! And more important, I could sing! Praise be, etc. I didn't know if it was a cold or what, but all I cared about was that it was over. A little part of me wondered if that day of loss was meant to remind me to appreciate my gifts and not take them for granted, and I didn't! I went back to my rehearsing with new gratitude, and for five days everything was just fine.

Then today I got up there on the stage, opened my mouth, and *nothing*. I came straight home, and Gramma Patty sent me to bed again. She says I pushed myself too hard and didn't give myself a chance to fully recover. Maybe it's true—I do feel kind of awful. Last time it was just my voice, like someone had flicked a switch and turned it off but left the rest of me just fine. This time it's definitely more than that. I feel . . . run-down. Exhausted. A little achy, maybe. I wonder if I have a slight fever. I had strange dreams last night, and this morning I felt so low, I actually thought about going to school without doing my ~divanation~. But I can't do that—you have to have standards. And it's what people expect from me. The whole school might become demoralized if I showed up in plain braids.

Gramma Patty just brought me some more tea, and now that I've written all this out, I'm feeling a little calmer. Maybe this is just a message that I've been pushing myself too hard, and I need to rest for a while. I'm going to sleep early tonight, and I'm going to take a whole week off from singing, even if my voice comes back. That should help, and one week isn't really going to set me back for the audition. I have to remember to take care of myself.

TUESDAY, JANUARY 14, 6:15 A.M. (PUBLIC)

I just had the most terrible nightmare. I don't even know how to describe it. I know, I know, no one ever wants to hear someone describe their dreams, but . . . this wasn't like a normal dream. Not even like a normal nightmare. It was so clear and vivid—not all mixed up and confusing, the way my dreams usually are.

There wasn't really any story to it. All I remember was I was strapped down so I couldn't move at all. At first I thought I was on some kind of bed, but it wasn't really a bed. . . . It was more of an iron grate. I wasn't scared or anything. I was just like, *Oh, I guess this is what's happening now.* But then I realized someone was lighting a fire under the grate. Under *me*. And it started to get hotter and hotter until I could feel the flames tickling my skin.

And it *hurt*. I thought things weren't supposed to hurt

in dreams! I don't think I've ever experienced pain in a dream before, except when something also hurt me in real life (like when I fell out of bed that one time). But this wasn't like that. It was like I was being burned all over my body, and I could *feel* it—my skin blistering and crackling like a roasted pig.

But I didn't scream. I didn't do anything to try to save myself. Not that there was much I could have done, but I don't remember crying or struggling. It was just me and that grate and the fire. And the pain.

Then I opened my eyes and I was in my bed. I never even had a sense of waking up. It was just like I'd been living through this horrible thing, with my eyes closed, and when I opened them, I was back to myself.

I don't know. I know it was just a dream, but it shook me up, I guess. It was just so real. Part of me still feels like it really happened, even though I know that's impossible.

That was weird.

I just got done writing up and posting my dream, but when I reloaded the page, there was this other post I don't remember making already on the blog. I mean, I *definitely* did not make that post. It was time-stamped from the middle of the night—when I was asleep!

It was just some weird photo. I have no clue where it came from. Some kind of glitch with the website, I guess? Wires crossed? ¯_(ツ)_/¯ I don't even know if that's possible, lol. But I don't know where else it could have come from, so I guess that must be it.

Anyway, I deleted it as soon as I saw it. I'm sorry if any of you out there saw it before I caught it! That's not the kind of thing I usually post at all.

I was going to just delete that photo from the other post, but I decided to save it first. Just in case it's not a glitch. Like if it's someone who has hacked my blog and is trying to mess with me, maybe. I don't know who would do that, but you never know. . . . All kinds of crazies out there.

I thought it might be smart to save it in a locked post in case I ever needed to show it as evidence or something.

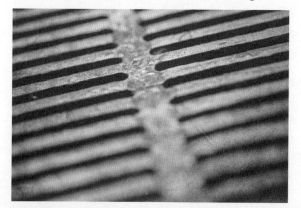

I didn't notice before, because I was panicking about a strange pic on my blog and whether it would upset people and cost me followers, but now that I look at it again, it kind of reminds me of my dream, and that metal grill I was strapped to. Isn't that strange? I mean, it must just be a coincidence. What else could it be? Gives me the shivers either way, though.

Hey, everyone!

I just wanted to let everybody know I'm doing okay. Thank you all for your concern. I have gotten soooo many nice messages from people since my last couple of posts. You guys are the best, seriously. I know I've been kind of down lately and not like myself—some of you were worried about that dream I had, and then there was that weirdness with the picture—but you don't have to worry. I'm getting better, and I'll be back to your regularly scheduled ~divanation~ posts before you know it.

It's nice to know you care—I love you all!

Also, I hate to bring this up, but to the people who felt the need to send anon messages complaining about the "turn this blog has taken" and threatening to unfollow . . . yeah, I didn't appreciate that. This blog is a labor of love, and I haven't been feeling well, so that means I haven't been able to post my usual stuff. If hearing real stuff about what's going on in my life bothers you so much, go ahead and unfollow. Fine by me.

Okay, sorry about that. It was only a few people, but it had to be said.

Thanks again for your notes and messages! I love you all.

FRIDAY, JANUARY 17, 10:15 P.M. (PRIVATE)

I'm so sick of my blog fans making me feel guilty for living my life and wanting to share it. I thought they all supported me, but they're only here for ~**laetitia**~, not the real me. I guess that shouldn't surprise me, but I wish I had someone to talk to about what's going on.

There's Mamma and Gramma, of course, but they don't really count. They're too full of opinions on how I should lead my life, plus they'll get all worked up and worried if they think something is really wrong. I've got my crew at school, but I guess I'm realizing now that I'm not all that close to any of them. We mostly just kid around, and I never have deep, serious conversations with them.

The people I know just aren't interested in the same stuff as I am. For as long as I can remember, all I've cared about is my singing. A lot of people think that's cool, but that doesn't mean they want to hear about the hours I spend practicing every day or the techniques I'm trying to develop or the recordings I'm listening to. If I talk about that stuff, people tune out after a few minutes and change the subject to something I don't know much about: parties or movies or sports. I've learned over the years to stay quiet and just laugh at other people's jokes.

I wish Angela were still around. I miss her so much! She always had time for me. She lived across the street when I first moved here, but she moved away last summer. We were about five when we met, and back then you could just walk up to another little girl playing in her yard and be like, *We're best friends now*, and that was that. It was simpler. I remember when I first realized I was going to be a singer, I told Angela that when she grew up, she could be my manager and we would always be together. I have no idea how I even knew about managers then. I must have heard some diva talking about hers in a TV interview or something. Angela and I both thought it sounded grown-up and impressive. We'd play for hours, me as the pop diva, and her managing me. She'd dress me up and show me how to move while I sang. We were a great team.

Then Angela's mom got a new boyfriend, and they moved to another neighborhood. And I know, it's not like they moved to the other side of the universe—it's just two short bus trips away—but she goes to a different high school, and we don't see each other every day, and it's just different. She texts me sometimes or we chat online, but we don't seem to have as much in common anymore. Angela got a boyfriend, and now all our conversations are just Tre this and Tre that. She doesn't seem interested in music. Maybe she never really was, and just did all that stuff for me.

We used to talk about anything and everything. I want to be able to go across the street and tell her all the crazy stuff that's been going on, and have her listen and reassure me that I'm not just making a big deal out of nothing.

SATURDAY, JANUARY 18, 10:30 A.M. (PRIVATE)

Oh great. Now I just lost a bunch of followers. Seriously, people? Folks are damn fickle. Oh well, who cares about them anyway? Haters, etc.

Maybe I shouldn't have posted so much about being sick or losing my voice. People don't like to hear about that sort of stuff, I guess. Or maybe it wasn't even that—maybe it was that last public post I made, complaining about the anon hate I was getting. People come here, expecting positivity and sweetness. I guess I better keep it that way.

Things *have* been getting a little gloomy around here. I need to post something more in my usual style to reassure people the blog hasn't changed. But I can't sing, and I'm just not up to the hair and makeup tutorials right now. Maybe an AMA? People usually like those.

SATURDAY, JANUARY 18, 10:45 A.M. (PUBLIC)

Feeling a bit better, but I'm still resting my voice. Since I'm just stuck here, moping about how I can't rehearse, maybe you all can entertain me. Ask Me Anything, starting now!

Hi, Laetitia! I really love your blog! You're so fierce and ambitious and driven, I just know you're going to be a big star one day. Can you talk a little bit about how you got started as a singer? Do you take lessons or have a voice coach?—anonymous

Thank you so much for the ask, Nonny! You're so sweet.

I can't believe I never told the story on here of how I got into singing, but I can't find it in my archives. I've been singing since I was a little girl. I got handpicked out of my church congregation to join the choir when I was only seven years old, because the choir director said even from the pews, she could hear I had a voice like an angel.

†_(°–°*)β <-- me. ;)

Since then, I've had more solos than anyone in the history of our church. I love it! Most teenagers probably think going to church is a pain in the you-know-what, but I look forward to Sundays all week long. I'm never more myself than when I'm performing for people.

My deep dark secret is . . . shhhhh . . . I wasn't a *bit* surprised when I got picked that day. I know, I know! You're not supposed to admit to stuff like that. You're supposed to be all humble, like . . . what??? Little old me? But I can't lie: that's never how it's been with me. I still remember the day the choir director approached Mamma and Gramma Patty after church, and how amazed they both were that their little baby girl had been picked out of the crowd, but to me, it felt inevitable. I felt like I'd always known this was coming.

I can't really explain it. As long as I can remember, I've always had this sense I would wind up doing something really big. Something that would make people all over the world know my name. I don't know where this certainty came from. . . . It's like a little voice inside me that has always whispered that I'm special, and it's only a matter of time before the rest of the world realizes it too. Does everyone feel this way? Maybe they do. Maybe we all feel like we're special and destined for some particular kind of greatness. And I guess in a way, that's true. We're all part of God's plan, and what could be greater than that?

But for me, it's always felt a little different. Mamma likes to tell a story from when I was a baby. She says I always loved it when people cooed over me and said, "That's the most beautiful baby I've ever seen" or "Aren't you the prettiest little girl in the world?" Mamma never thought much of it. Then one day in the

21

grocery store, I heard an old woman tell some other little girl she was the sweetest thing in the whole wide world, and I went right up to the woman and said, "No, she isn't. I am!"

←~ (o ` ▽´)oΨ *devil grin*

I was only three when it happened, so Mamma and Gramma Patty mostly just thought it was cute, and didn't make too much of it. And I learned pretty quickly you're not supposed to say that stuff out loud. But the truth is, I still feel that way sometimes. Maybe I'm not the prettiest or the sweetest or whatever, but that little voice telling me I have a special destiny has never gone away.

For a while I wasn't sure what it would be. I thought maybe I would be an adventurer and travel the world or I'd cure some disease or be president. But the day that church lady spoke to Mamma and Gramma Patty, I knew I was born to be a singer. My voice was the thing that made me special, and someday everyone in the world would be able to see me the way I had always seen myself.

But of course that doesn't mean I've just been sitting here, waiting for the world to beat a path to my door! I know it doesn't work like that. *I* may have always known I was special, but if I'm going to convince the rest of the world, I know I have to pay my dues and put some real work in. So even as a little kid, I practiced every day. I just started singing all the time, and I'd sing along with my favorite songs, and every time I found a note I couldn't hit or a rhythm I couldn't copy, I'd work and work at it until I did. I've never had a teacher or a coach, other than the church choir director, but I know I've worked as hard as any singer out there.

And thanks to that, my voice is so much stronger and clearer than it used to be. My pitch is more accurate, my range extended. I know there are still better singers in the world than I am, but I think I'm ready for my shot now. I want the world to hear me! But I just have to be patient a little while longer, and practice and train all I can, so when my chance comes, I can really blow them away.

SATURDAY, JANUARY 18, 12:30 P.M. (PUBLIC)

I love your style and aesthetic, and your voice is so beautiful. Do you ever write your own songs? It would probably help you get your big break if you did. It seems like all the biggest singers write their own lyrics.—[username redacted]

Thank you—you are so sweet! Actually, there is a long tradition of singers and songwriters being two separate callings. A lot of my idols never wrote a word or a note, but they put so much passion into their singing that it became an art form. Right now I want to focus on training my voice, because I feel like that's what I have to offer the world. Other people may have the gift of writing lyrics or composing, but maybe they can't sing. We all have our callings, and mine is to give a voice to the words and music that might be someone else's calling.

˚ · ✿ ヾ\(｡◕‿◕｡)/✿ · ˚

SATURDAY, JANUARY 18, 12:42 P.M. (PRIVATE)

I think that's the third (fourth?) time someone has asked me on the blog why I don't write my own songs. It's pretty annoying, to be honest. Yes, I realize that's the fashion now, but I don't know how! It's not that I haven't tried coming up with some lyrics; it's just that they're all terrible. I mean really bad. I don't even know what to write about. In church we sing all these praise songs, and they're beautiful, but there's nothing I could add to those. I'd be ashamed if I wrote something silly and stupid and then tried to offer it to God. That doesn't seem right.

And then there are love songs, which are what most pop songs are and what most people want to listen to, but it's not like I have a lot of experience in that area. I can't write about deep, passionate love. And besides, I'd be way too embarrassed to sing about anything so personal. I like singing, not writing—what's wrong with that? I have one gift, and I just want to make it the best I can. Why does everyone want me to be something I'm not?

My week of rest is almost up, and I have been *really* good about going to bed early every night, eating well, and not singing, not even in the shower. Hopefully, when I start rehearsing again this week, everything will be back to normal!

Except I'm not sure I'm getting better. I don't exactly *feel* better. I thought, after all this rest, I would be full of energy, but even though I try to fight it, I feel worse than ever. I've been dragging myself through school every day, like --> (₀-_-₀).

I've also been kind of sick to my stomach all week, except when it lets up for a bit and I'm suddenly *starving*. What is this? The flu? I really hope it gets better soon. Maybe I've been resting *too* much, and that's what's making me feel bad. I just need to get back to rehearsing, and I'm sure I'll feel better.

By the way, thank you all for your thoughts and prayers—it means so much to me to have your support. Sorry I haven't felt up to posting any hair and makeup tutorials lately. I'm just too worn-down.

angela: hey. you there?

laetitia: hey, girl! i was just thinking about you the other day!

laetitia: i miss you so much!

angela: i miss you too.

angela: i saw tre talking to another girl today. i don't know what to do.

laetitia: about what?

angela: about tre!

laetitia: oh. he was just talking to her, right? that doesn't seem like that big a deal.

angela: maybe. that's what lisa said. but then tasha said tre's only been with me less than a month, and he shouldn't even be looking at other girls when he could be looking at me.

laetitia: i guess.

angela: or am i just making a huge deal out of nothing?

laetitia: maybe . . . ?

angela: well, which is it??? geez, don't you even have an opinion?

laetitia: come on. you know i don't know about this stuff. plus i'm not feeling well.

angela: why, what's wrong?

laetitia: lost my voice.

angela: what? like, you're sick?

laetitia: idk. i can talk, still. . . . it's just my singing voice. i can't sing *at all*.

angela: wow, that sucks. worried about your audition? you're still doing that, right?

laetitia: hope so. idk. not if my voice doesn't come back.

laetitia: plus it's not just that. i've been having these really scary dreams. only . . .

angela: what?

laetitia: don't call me crazy, okay?

angela: ha-ha, of course not.

laetitia: sometimes i wake up with, like, bruises or sores where i got hurt during my dream. and they hurt really bad when i press on them. sort of a burning feeling.

angela: maybe don't press on them??

laetitia: ha-ha. yeah, that makes sense.

angela: don't worry, babe. you'll be fine. you're just anxious about your audition, but you're gonna be great! you always are.

laetitia: thanks.

angela: oh no, tre's online. should i talk to him?

laetitia: idk . . . probably?

angela: okay, i'm going to ask him about that girl. talk later!

TUESDAY, JANUARY 21, 4:40 P.M. (PUBLIC)

I guess I really must be exhausted still. I think I fell asleep on the bus. I've never done that before. Usually I'm up, chattering away with people or texting with Mamma or listening to music. Today I couldn't seem to do anything but just sit there and stare out the window. Then, one second I was looking out the window at the streets I've seen a million times before, and the next, I guess my eyes had closed, because the scene was totally different. There was a crowd of people all yelling at me. I couldn't make out the words, but I knew they were saying terrible things about me, like I had committed some awful crime. In front of me, lying flat on a platform, there was a giant wheel, like maybe for an old wagon or something . . . only there were sharp spikes all over it.

Then I was grabbed from behind and turned around, and the next thing I knew, I was being strapped across this wheel.

I knew I was being punished for my crime, and even though I couldn't remember what I had done, I didn't fight or struggle. I just accepted that I deserved the punishment, like last time.

That's when they started beating me. I couldn't see who—I don't know if I had closed my eyes in the dream or if I was too focused on the pain to notice anything else. I'm not sure I've ever felt something so awful. They were beating my arms and legs with hammers and clubs, and I could feel the bones shattering under the skin.

I don't know how long I sat there like that. The bus ride isn't long, but I'm not sure if it was, like, a second or a couple of minutes. In the dream, it felt like forever. It felt like days. I was just lost in pain and hopelessness.

Who knows how long it might have gone on like that, except one of my friends said she noticed me sitting there, whimpering and crying a little, my eyes closed. She touched my shoulder and asked if I was okay, and I snapped out of it. The weird thing is, I wasn't slumped down in my seat like I was sleeping. She said I had been sitting up straight, my whole body rigid and twitching. And when my eyes snapped open, for a second I didn't even know who she was. I felt like I'd been in another world.

So weird to have two of these dreams in a row like this. Are they related to my other problems? If all this is really just the flu, then I guess maybe they could be fever dreams. Except I don't feel like I have a fever.

TUESDAY, JANUARY 21, 3:50 P.M. (PRIVATE)

What is this??? Another weird photo? I just posted that thing about my dream, and it was there. I think I caught it and locked it up as a private post before anyone saw it. Lord, this is the last thing I need to deal with right now. It can't just be a glitch, can it? I dream about being tortured on an iron grill, and a picture of a grill appears. I dream about being beaten within an inch of my life on some wheel, and this shows up? Someone must be reading my posts and then hacking into my account to mess with me. But how? And why? I've never done anything to hurt or offend anyone, I don't think.

Also, both times these pictures have looked like they were posted *before* I made my dream descriptions. How could that be? Is my secret enemy psychic or something? It can't be that. They must just be playing with the time stamps somehow.

It's really creeping me out, though. This blog has always been a safe space for me, where I can get support and encouragement. It used to be a great pick-me-up when I'd had a bad day, to come on here and see people liking and reblogging my stuff and sending me fan mail. It made me feel like I was worth something. It's awful for someone to attack it like this now, when I'm already feeling scared and sick and helpless.

I'm not sure what to do. I guess I'll send a message to the support staff, to see if they can tell me what's going on. And in the meantime, I'll change my password. Maybe that will help.

I just realized I lost a bunch more followers this week. Nice. Let people see a side of you that is anything but cheerful and upbeat, and they start to jump ship. I wonder if this has anything to do with that photo. I thought I had caught it quickly, but maybe some people did see it and then decide I've lost it. It probably doesn't help that it's been a while since I've posted normal photos, like selfies.

People see one thing they don't like, and they are so quick to unfollow! It should have been obvious it was a mistake or a glitch and nothing to do with me. Anyone who's been following me for a while knows I do *not* post stuff like that. You'd think they'd give me the benefit of the doubt, or maybe message me to ask if I'm feeling okay.

Maybe I should have been keeping up better with my

in-box. There are a bunch of messages in there about the dream I posted. Some of my followers are just concerned, but of course I can't get away from assholes who are like, *I followed you for makeup tips; I am not interested in your creepy-ass dreams*. Thanks for your support! Maybe it was dumb to post that kind of thing. I know everyone always hates dream posts—I've made fun of them myself—but I thought these were more interesting. Well, they were interesting to *me*. And isn't this journal supposed to be about me and my life?

Ha. That's not how anyone else sees it.

Maybe I better make another video, or at least post some selfies, before I lose any more followers. People are used to things being positive and uplifting around here. I guess if I ever want to talk about my not-so-good days, I should stick to private posts.

SATURDAY, JANUARY 25, 9:10 A.M. (PUBLIC)

Still resting my voice! But I thought I'd share a few pics of my look for today. I'll write up instructions for it soon, I swear.

[photo redacted]
[photo redacted]
[photo redacted]

Hope you like it! If so, show me some love! My ask box is always open.

Hi, Laetitia! I just want to say that you are my style *icon*. I love that you are representing for beautiful, proud black women. I was just wondering: how did you get started wearing colored wigs? Did you just go for it one day, or was it more of a gradual thing? And what do you do on days when you don't have the time or energy for all that styling?—[username redacted]

Are you suggesting I was not *born* with different color hair every day??

(✿◡◡)

Jkjk. You're right: there is an origin story to this look. When I was a little kid, I wore my hair in braids, like all the other girls in my classes. Then one summer I went away to camp and I came home with a bad case of head lice, and Mamma had to shave off all my hair. I cried and cried! My head didn't feel right, and whenever I looked in the mirror, I didn't recognize myself.

Gramma Patty tried to make me feel better by wrapping my head in scarves, which helped. Then one day I was watching some cartoon where the heroine had beautiful sparkly purple hair, and I turned to Mamma and I said that when my hair grew back, I wanted it to look like that. And Mamma smiled and said I didn't have to wait for it. She walked me to the store, and right in the toy aisle they had this bright pink costume wig with sparkly strands in it. It was cheap and tacky and ugly as sin, but I fell in love with it.

I wore it every day for a month, until it fell to pieces. I cried over it, but for my birthday, Mamma got me another—better quality this time. And that's how it began.

Right from the beginning, it changed so much about me. I loved the way people noticed me in school. People could finally see on the outside how special I'd always felt on the inside. Eventually I moved on to fancier, better-made wigs, though they're all synthetic. I save up and get new ones on birthdays and holidays. And after a while I started experimenting with makeup, too, to complete the look.

We're all starring in the TV show of our lives, and I want to be a real ~*☆star☆*~. When I started making myself up that way, some folks thought I was crazy; some folks threw shade. But mostly it made people take me more seriously when I said I was going to be a ~*pop diva*~ when I grew up. Like they could see it now.

The only person who still doesn't love it is Gramma Patty. Most days she lets it slide, but I know she doesn't approve. She says it's prideful, and that I should be happy with the hair and face God gave me. That I should dress more modestly, instead of trying to look like a peacock all the time. But Mamma is on my side. She's always had a flair for the dramatic, and everyone says I get it from her. She says if my body is a temple, then putting on some extra decorations is a way of honoring and celebrating it. And she says if it makes me happy, it makes God happy too. But who knows what makes God happy? I'll worry about that in the next life. This life is for me.

Something is really wrong. What is going on with me? I didn't want to make too big a deal out of a couple of nightmares, because I knew if I tried to tell Mamma or Gramma Patty about them, they'd just brush them off as bad dreams. I mean, I know they'd care and be sympathetic, but what are you going to do about a bad dream? Everyone gets them sometimes, especially if you're not sleeping well when you're sick. I could already hear Gramma Patty's voice in my head, saying something sensible like that. And I tried to convince myself that was the truth. However scary it felt from the inside, a nightmare is really no big deal. Even one you have in the middle of the day that makes you cry from very real pain.

But this is different. I definitely wasn't asleep this time. I was in the shower! Everything was basically normal, except I'd been feeling a little sick to my stomach, but that's not unusual these days. I closed my eyes to wash my hair, and there it was. I didn't exactly see anything, but I became overcome by this intense fear that someone was going to kill me. And I'm just standing there, quietly freaking out, and then I feel . . . I don't know what the hell it was, but I've never felt pain like that. I seriously thought I'd just been shot in the leg. Except that's crazy, right? How do you get shot in the shower? The shower door was still there, and it's not like there are any windows.

I would have fallen over right then, but something was supporting me. I felt my muscles and bones give way, but instead of sinking to the floor of the shower, I just sort of hung there, as if invisible ropes were holding me up. Then there was another shot, this time in my hip. And another in my shoulder. I thought I would faint from the pain.

Finally I couldn't take it anymore, and I cried out. More like shrieked, actually. Mamma and Gramma Patty came barging in to see if I was okay, and that's when I finally opened my eyes. The other times, opening my eyes made everything okay again. The world went back to normal and the pain went away. But not this time. I looked down, and there was blood everywhere. Right where I'd felt those shots. Not just blood—I could see things sticking out of me, like wooden rods. Like I'd been shot through with arrows.

When I saw that, I really started screaming. And Mamma was trying to calm me down, and I was babbling at her, trying to explain what had happened, except how could I possibly explain it? Then I looked down again and there was no blood. There were no arrows. Not even a mark anywhere on my skin. Just me, standing there, shivering and naked, the shower still running, and Mamma trying to calm me down and get me into a robe.

What must she think of me now? She must think I've lost my mind. And why should I think any different? This doesn't happen to normal people. I saw in her eyes how worried she was, but she didn't want to scare me. She just put me to bed and told me to relax and get some rest.

I tried to sleep, but every time I closed my eyes, I kept seeing that blood again, and those arrows, long and thick, sticking out of me. So I got up and decided to write about it. Maybe that will help shake those images free from my brain.

This time, I'm just going to post this as a locked entry. That way my little stalker troll won't be able to mess with my head by posting some picture of whatever is scaring me. It's no big loss. I don't think any of my followers really like hearing about this stuff, anyway.

SATURDAY, JANUARY 25, 10:25 P.M. (PRIVATE)

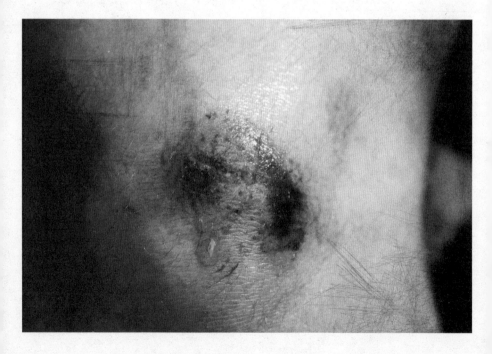

Holy Jesus . . .

How is that even possible? It happened again, just like before: one minute I hit post; the next minute I go to my blog to see the new post and there's a photo waiting for me. I swear, it wasn't there before, but the time stamp is from right when I was in the shower. Right when I was having that . . . whatever it was.

I just switched the post to private, but it posted as public originally, which means more people saw it. And this photo isn't just weird and random; it's really disturbing. People are going to have conniptions in my message box over this. I guess I better apologize again! This is becoming a habit. Who's even going to believe at this point that it's not my fault? They probably all think I'm doing this on purpose.

I just don't understand it. How can this troll still be messing with me? Where are these pictures coming from??? And why does it always seem like they're pictures from inside my own head? It's almost like my thoughts are projecting them onto my blog. But that's *really* crazy.

I need to tell someone what's going on, but I don't even know how to describe it.

I'm really, really sorry—to anyone who might have seen that horrible picture. I swear, I had nothing to do with it! I've changed my password and sent e-mails to the support staff, but nothing seems to help. Has anyone else out there had this problem? Has the site been acting up for you all in other ways? Or does anyone have experience with hackers that might be helpful? I'm kind of desperate at this point.

Anyway, I'm really sorry if anyone saw that and was traumatized by it. Believe me, I feel the same way. I will totally understand if any of you feel like you have to unfollow me after that. I wish I could guarantee there will never be anything like that on this blog again, but at this point . . . I don't know if I can.

SUNDAY, JANUARY 26, 9:18 A.M. (PRIVATE)

So I switched the default posting style for this blog to private. That way, if any more of the creepy photos appear, at least I'll be the only one who sees them. I think, in a way, they're not meant for my followers. They're really meant for me.

I just can't deal with worrying all the time if some horrible picture is going to pop up while I'm not looking, and get people all upset. Besides, there isn't much point in my having a public blog these days. I'm not singing, and I can't be bothered to do ~divanation~ tutorials anymore. I just have other stuff on my mind. And my followers let me know loud and clear that they're not interested in the stuff I've been dealing with lately. All those people who I thought were my friends and fans, people I thought loved and admired me, they're pretty much all gone now, except for a handful that are probably all bots or abandoned blogs.

Anyway, I'm tired of writing for them and trying to keep them happy. I don't have the space in my mind right now to worry about that stuff, and I don't really feel like sharing. I need someplace to work through what's going on in my life, and I don't need hundreds of people watching me while I do it. Maybe someday I'll feel comfortable writing publicly again, like if my voice comes back, but for now I feel better and safer this way.

You know what's weird, though? I keep logging in just to look at those bizarre photos. I saved them all because I thought it was a good idea to keep a record of them, but now, even though they really upset me at first, I find myself fascinated by them.

It's so strange, because I *never* went looking for stuff like that before. I know some people enjoy gory or scary or weird things, but that wasn't me. I only wanted stuff in my life that made me feel happy and positive and joyful. So why am I drawn to them now? Well, I guess it kind of makes sense—it's not every day you get to see pictures from the inside of your own head.

Wow. Is that really what I think it is? I know I said that before, but it can't honestly be that, right? Still, I don't know what else it is. I've spent hours online, trying to find the source of these pictures. Looking for anyone on this site or any other who took the original photo, or even just reblogged it. But I can't find them anywhere. It's like they materialized out of the air. Or, like I said before, out of my brain. But no, I don't even want to think about that. It's too creepy.

MONDAY, JANUARY 27, 6:15 P.M. (PRIVATE)

I fainted in school today. I'm not even sure how it happened. I've just been feeling so bad lately. I was climbing the stairs to go to biology and I was feeling queasy, but that's nothing new. Then my vision went black and my knees were wobbly, and it was like I was back in those dreams again, except all the pain was coming at me together. Burning, beating, piercing, all coming over me in waves.

The next thing I knew, I was waking up on the floor, a crowd of people around me, and I had a nasty bump on my head. Gramma Patty had to come pick me up from the nurse's office and take me home. She sent me up to bed, even though I was already feeling a lot better. Then when Mamma got home from work, she made such a fuss! She asked me, like, a million questions about how I've been feeling, and am I tender or sore anywhere, and what have I eaten, even though she knows very well what I eat, since we eat most of our meals together.

Then finally she came out with it. What she'd been hinting at ever since she got home. She asked me if I was pregnant. Me! Of course I got all embarrassed and was like, *Mamma, I don't even have a boyfriend.* Then she pointed out that you don't exactly need a boyfriend to get pregnant. She didn't have a boyfriend when she had me. Fine, yes, point taken. But this is different. I tried to convince her that my having a baby was a biological impossibility, but it barely slowed her down. She just kept ranting about me throwing away all my dreams over some boy, and how she had prayed and prayed I wouldn't make the same mistakes she did, and I have so much potential, and on and on and on. Finally I told her I'd let Gramma Patty take me to the doctor tomorrow to get checked out, just to put her mind at ease. Maybe a doctor can at least help me figure out what this is and why my voice has been so unreliable lately. Mamma is fixated on the whole pregnancy thing, but honestly I'm scared it's something much worse.

laetitia: angela, you there?

angela: yeah, i've been meaning to talk to you. i found out about that girl tre was talking to.

angela: it's his ex-girlfriend's little sister. doesn't that seem suspicious?

laetitia: idk. maybe. listen, can we talk? something really weird just happened.

angela: what's up?

laetitia: i passed out in school today.

angela: omg! are you okay?

laetitia: i think so, but that's not even the weird part. after i came to, i started to feel better, but my skin felt all weird and itchy. this weird sharp and itchy feeling in places all over my body. i tried to ignore it, but it kept bothering me.

    angela: what is it? a rash or something?

    laetitia: that's what i thought. so when i got home, i got undressed to take a shower, and i immediately felt better, except i had these weird pink sores on my skin. and i picked up my clothes and shook them, and look what came out.

    angela: laetitia, what is this?

    laetitia: what does it look like?

    angela: it looks like a pile of feathers. are you saying there were feathers in your clothes?

laetitia: i don't know! i mean, i guess so. but where could they have come from?

angela: lol, i have no idea. maybe someone stuffed some feathers down your shirt while you were passed out.

laetitia: omg, seriously? who would do that?

angela: i don't know. what else could it be?

angela: you still there?

laetitia: yeah.

laetitia: don't laugh, okay?

angela: okay . . .

laetitia: i sort of feel like they came out of my skin.

angela: laetitia.

angela: what?

angela: i'm not laughing. but you know that's crazy, right?

laetitia: i know how it sounds, yeah. idk, maybe it is crazy. i just needed to tell someone. my gramma patty is taking me to the doctor. . . . should i tell her about it?

angela: no.

laetitia: what? why not?

angela: because the doctor will think you are legit crazy! you can't go around telling people you're turning into a damn bird.

laetitia: i didn't say that!

angela: you wanted my advice, right? don't tell the doctor; don't tell anyone. just ignore it. someone probably did something with the feathers to mess with you, and your imagination got carried away.

laetitia: you really think so?

angela: yeah. listen, i'm your friend, and you can trust me. but don't tell this story to anyone else unless you want them to think you've lost your damn mind.

Surprise, surprise, the doctor says I'm not pregnant! This was not exactly news to me, but at least it gets Mamma off my back. As for what *is* going on with my body, no real help there. Dr. Afolabi looked at my throat and said it seems a little irritated, even though my white blood cells look normal. She said to keep gargling with salt water, make sure I'm eating and sleeping enough, and I should feel better soon. They're doing some tests for thyroid stuff and an iron deficiency and I don't remember what else, so maybe those will turn something up. I can't decide if that would make me feel better or worse. She asked me if I had any other symptoms, and I almost told her about the strange bruises and sores, but then I remembered how Angela had reacted to the feathers, and I decided not to even go down that road. They've faded by now, anyway.

I guess all I can do now is try to get some sleep and hope I don't have any more weird nightmares.

WEDNESDAY, FEBRUARY 5, 4:20 P.M. (PRIVATE)

Haven't written in a while. I've been avoiding this journal
because I didn't want to admit what's going on. I thought if
I just acted like everything was normal, things might actually
be normal. I didn't want to admit things are getting worse, not
better.

I feel *really* sick lately. Not just when I wake up, but all the
time, which is making it hard to eat right. Even looking at food
makes me want to puke my guts up, though I've only given in
a couple of times. And I'm tired *all* the time, and sleeping ten
or even twelve hours a night. This isn't like me at all! I don't
understand what's the matter.

The doctor's blood tests all came back normal. The weird
thing is, if I didn't know who I'd been spending my nights with
(no one), I'd almost start to wonder if I *were* pregnant. I defi-

nitely feel . . . I don't know. Different. I get hot and cold flashes, or I feel like little bolts of electricity are shooting through me. Or like there's a strange thrumming beneath my skin. It feels like I'm changing, or growing somehow.

And through all this, I still don't understand what's going on with my singing voice. It's not like the first time. My speaking voice is fine, but when I go to sing . . . Well, I guess it's a little better than it was. It's not that nothing comes out, but the most I can do is a kind of throaty, breathy warble. It's not at all like my usual crystal-clear pitch. And I can hardly produce more than a whisper, when I used to be able to belt big enough to fill the whole church, even without a microphone.

Last Sunday I had to sit out during choir again, and after church the director told me she assigned my solo parts to someone else. She seemed really apologetic, and she said I could have my spot back as soon as I was feeling better. I know she's just doing what she has to do, and I tried to be mature about it in front of her, but when I got home, I just cried and cried. Mamma and Gramma Patty didn't even try to make me talk about it or cheer me up. They understood I needed to let myself be sad about it for a while.

Thursday, February 6, 4:30 P.M. (Private)

I did something strange when I was walking home from the bus stop today. I saw this dead animal lying in the road, and I stopped to look at it. Is that weird? Normally if I saw something like that, I'd shudder and look away as fast as I could, and just keep walking and try not to think about it. Like Mamma says, there's no point in inviting negativity into your life. Better to stay focused on the positive.

But today, I don't know. Maybe it's because I haven't been feeling well, but I was drawn to the animal. And as I looked at it, I realized it reminded me of something I couldn't quite place. Actually it kind of reminded me of those weird pictures that have been appearing on my blog. I don't know why—it didn't look anything like those pictures—but something about this dead animal just brought those other images back to my mind. Like they were *connected* somehow.

And as soon as I'd had that thought, I pulled out my phone and started taking pictures of it. I never do that. Pretty much the only photos I ever take are selfies to post on my blog. I'm very good at that, getting all my best angles and the best lighting and everything, but I don't know the first thing about photographing anything else. But for some reason I just wanted to take this image home with me and preserve it.

When I got home, the first thought I had was to post it up on my blog. But that's a terrible idea! I've just spent all this time and energy trying to reassure people that those weird pictures that kept showing up had *nothing* to do with me, and now I want to add to them? It doesn't even make sense, but it was this weird urge. I don't know. I guess I just wanted to share it with someone. I wanted to know if other people saw something strange and beautiful in it too.

But all my posts are private now anyway, so I wound up showing it to Gramma Patty instead, because she was sitting in the kitchen when I got home. She said it was disgusting, and she didn't know why I'd want to waste my time on something ugly and twisted. So that's that, I guess.

She's right, though. I don't know what I thought I was doing. I don't know why I'd even want something so morbid on my blog! I've always used this blog as a place for inspiration and positivity, to help me reach all my goals. I don't know how some gross animal carcass is supposed to help me with any of that.

Thursday, February 6, 11:06 P.M. (Private)

I've been thinking more about that picture I posted. I'm still not sure why I was drawn to something that is so *not me*, but maybe that's exactly what I liked about it. I've always had a really strong sense of who I am—more than most teenagers, I think. I'm a singer; my voice is who I am. It's what people know me for; it's why people like me.

But now that my voice isn't so reliable, what does that say about me? About my identity? It's like my whole sense of self is falling apart.

So, in a weird way, doing something so different from normal for me is kind of a comfort, like maybe there's a way I can continue to exist, even without my voice. Though I'm not sure what sort of life photographing dead animals prepares me for. . . .

SUNDAY, FEBRUARY 9, 8:16 A.M. (PRIVATE)

I tried to plead illness to get out of church today, but Mamma and Gramma Patty are making me go. The truth is, it hurts to go and watch everyone else perform when I know I should be up there with them. What's the point of church if I can't sing?

I mean, I believe in God. But it feels . . . distant. For Mamma, if the bus is two minutes late, or if they have the flavor of ice cream she likes at the store, that's all God speaking directly to her. And Gramma Patty, she hardly gets up to do the dishes without praying about it first. When I was a kid, I thought that was normal. It was the only thing I knew. But I've kind of outgrown it now, and it's just not how I see the world. Worrying about God is like worrying about politics—a lot of people take it really seriously, but ultimately I can't change anything, and none of it is going to make a difference in my life anyway. So what's the point of going to church every week? To prove to God you're a good person? Surely He has more important things to think about.

When I tried that argument, Gramma Patty said church isn't for God; it's for you. It's for people to find a bit of peace and calm before they start the week, to help them find strength and focus on what's important. Maybe that makes sense for her, but I just don't feel I get a lot out of it. On the other hand, I don't have it in me right now to start a fight about it, so I guess I'll just go. I'll try not to cringe when Chrissie Mathers screeches out *my* solo.

SUNDAY, FEBRUARY 9, 11:17 A.M. (PRIVATE)

Well, I'm glad I let them drag me to church. In all my angst-
ing over losing my place in the choir, I forgot there's another
reason to spend my Sundays in that overheated hall: cute
boys. One cute boy in particular. His name's Malcolm, and I
see him around school. Sometimes I even catch his eye, but
usually I'm so busy with choir stuff at church that I don't
have any chance to interact with him. This time, I was moping around with Mamma and Gramma Patty as they made
the usual after-church rounds, saying hi to everyone from the
neighborhood, when I realized Malcolm was standing right
next to me. I couldn't think of anything to say. He asked me
what I thought of the sermon, and I honestly had not been
paying attention at all. I'd just been brooding about the girl
who'd taken my place in the choir, whose voice is definitely

not as good as mine, and who really has no sense of style or flair whatsoever.

I couldn't exactly admit that to Malcolm. I don't know him well, but I sort of remembered he's a very serious person, if you know what I mean. He follows the news and politics, and he has a lot of opinions on "the world situation." I'm no airhead, but with everything I put into singing and my dreams for a career, I just don't have a ton of time or energy for that stuff. But I do have time for cute boys! So I did my best to keep up with him. I racked my brain and remembered the pastor had been talking about this trial that's been in the news a bunch. I've heard Mamma and Gramma Patty talk about it a few times too, but I was only half paying attention. It's something to do with Dwayne Robinson, who grew up not too far from here, just a couple of neighborhoods over. My high school's sports teams play his. He was shot dead a couple of months ago by police, and the whole city has been in an uproar ever since. They even put the cops on trial for murder. But that's all I really remembered.

So Malcolm was asking me what I thought of the sermon, and I was like, "It was okay, I guess. Pretty good. Made sense." I was trying not to say anything too specific and give away that I had hardly been paying attention, but that was apparently the wrong answer, because Malcolm got this look and was like, "Pretty good?"

I guess the point of the sermon had been that everyone should stay calm and let the justice system do its job, and just pray justice takes its course. It seemed to me like a pretty reasonable position, but not according to Malcolm. He said the last thing we can expect from the legal system is justice, and history suggests we can't much trust God, either. That struck me as a pretty nervy thing to say in church. Lucky for him, he wasn't standing near his mother, because I know she would have smacked him on the back of the head for talking like that.

Then Malcolm said, "We better get ready, because if the jury doesn't come back with a guilty verdict, the whole city is going to go up in flames."

That seemed a little excessive to me. How is violence going to help violence? And don't we have to trust the system to do its job?

But Malcolm looked pretty unimpressed by that argument. He said the police are just going to keep murdering innocent kids until the people rise up and do something about it. So I asked, "How can you be sure he's innocent? We weren't there. We can't know what really happened that night."

He just stared at me and then asked, "You haven't watched the video?" I felt dumb then because, once he mentioned it, I remembered I'd heard people talking about it. I saw links to it online and stuff. But no, I'd never clicked through and watched it, because it seemed too morbid. I usually avoid anything that might be violent or sad or upsetting. And it didn't have anything to do with me. I don't know! I had other stuff on my mind.

But now that I'm not singing, I guess I don't have so much other stuff to occupy me. And I am kind of curious what Malcolm was talking about. I guess I could check it out.

SUNDAY, FEBRUARY 9, 11:55 A.M. (PRIVATE)

I just watched the video.

Lord . . . now I feel really bad about that conversation with Malcolm. I don't know how anyone can pretend not to see what's going on in the video. Basically, Dwayne is sitting on his front steps when the cops roll up and get out of their car and start asking him questions. They say they received a call, and he says he doesn't know anything about that. He's got a paper bag set between his knees, and one cop asks, "What's in the bag?" and Dwayne says, "What?" The cop asks again: "What's in the bag?" and Dwayne says, "It's peanuts." He reaches into the bag to show them, and the next thing you can see, he's lying there, shot in the chest.

Turns out, the bag was full of peanuts. The cops were

answering a domestic violence complaint, but they had the wrong address.

I'm not sure when I've ever seen anything so awful. I can't help but feel like a shallow idiot, spending my whole life thinking about myself and my singing and my dreams, and completely ignoring what's going on around me. Something like this can happen right in my own community, and I just think, *Oh, that has nothing to do with me.*

It's got me wondering, *Is it completely selfish and pointless to devote my life to singing?* I've always assumed singing was what I was put on Earth to do. Why would God give me this voice if He didn't want me to use it? But now I'm not so sure. What if singing is a distraction? Or what if God didn't give it to me at all? People noticed my voice when I was a little kid, but to be honest, it wasn't all that great then. Just good for a kid. What really made me a strong singer was how much I practiced—rehearsing and rehearsing every day, sometimes for hours. And listening to other singers, experimenting with different techniques, all kinds of stuff like that. God didn't do that; *I* did that. What if it was all a waste of time?

But on the other hand, people have been singing in churches for hundreds, even thousands of years. There must be a reason for that. And I see it when I look out at the congregation, or even when I look around me at people's faces when I go to a pop concert. It gives people joy. Hope, even. People want to live in this world because there are songs in it. And that's not such a bad thing, is it?

I feel very confused right now. If I'm meant to be singing, why can't I sing anymore? And if I'm meant to be doing something else, what is it? I can't do anything for Dwayne now, and

I'm not sure what I could do to stop more things like that from happening in the future. Malcolm seems to have everything all figured out, but I just don't know. And what if I'm not "meant to be" doing anything at all? I believe in God because I always have, and I know it's important to Mamma and Gramma Patty, but for myself? It's not like I have any proof. If I'm honest with myself, I can imagine a world in which there is no God. It doesn't even bother me that much. But then, if this is all there is, what's the point of it all? What if there is no point?

Ugh, I'm giving myself a headache. Enough deep thoughts for tonight. I need to get some sleep.

TUESDAY, FEBRUARY 11, 9:30 P.M. (PRIVATE)

I don't want to jinx myself, but I've been feeling a little better the last couple of days. I still have that weird thrumming feeling under my skin, but now it's less connected to feeling queasy and light-headed. It feels more like a kind of energy, like I'm warming up to run a race. It's definitely easier to get up in the mornings. I'm still too nervous to try out my voice, though. I get so worried I'll open my mouth and nothing will come out, it seems easier just to not try.

I'm thinking about it, though.

The shower is so weirdly gross these days. Mamma is in an all-out war with the mildew on the shower door. She goes in and washes it down with bleach or ammonia or whatever chemical she can think of to get rid of it. Then I jump into a nice, shiny clean shower, and an hour later that gross gunk is back worse than ever. Mamma is pissed about it! She says nothing should be able to survive after what she sprayed in there, but I keep bringing it back to life somehow.

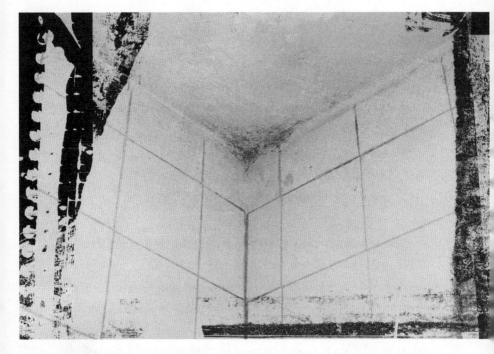

FRIDAY, FEBRUARY 14, 4:34 P.M. (PRIVATE)

I sang a few times this week. Not like old times, but I did have *some* voice at least. Maybe it's getting stronger.

I don't know. I'm trying so hard to stay optimistic and look on the bright side of everything, like Gramma Patty says. She says sulking around about how bad things are never helped anyone. And since the doctor seems to think my problem is all in my head, then if I can just force myself to be cheerful and upbeat, I'll be able to make myself better. That's the theory, anyway.

But I'm not sure I can do it. My voice is better, but it's not what it was, and at this rate I don't know how I'm going to prepare for that audition. I still feel weird all the time. Sometimes it's a good kind of weird, and sometimes it feels bad, and sometimes it's just . . . weird, and I don't know *how* to describe it.

This morning I woke up from bad dreams and had this

awful pain in my side, sort of over my ribs. It was like before, with the weird visions, except this time it felt like all the pain from those had been concentrated into this one spot, burning, breaking, piercing. I was convinced there must be some horrible wound or injury there, but when I lifted up my pajama top, it looked totally normal, though when I touched it, the pain was so awful, I nearly passed out. But after a minute of deep breathing, my ribs started to feel better.

I don't know if this is related to the other stuff, or something else entirely. It's not bothering me too much now though, at least.

Also, I took some more pictures on the way home from school. I'm kind of getting into this photography thing. It's not the same as singing—it doesn't feel like the kind of thing that will make me a ~*star*~—but it's interesting, and it makes me look around my neighborhood with new eyes. I see all kinds of weirdly beautiful things I never noticed before.

SATURDAY, FEBRUARY 15, 5:34 P.M. (PRIVATE)

I saw Renee today. She always manages to cheer me up. She had to cancel last month's appointment for something and we never managed to reschedule, so I guess it had been longer than usual since I've seen her.

Renee feels like the cool aunt I never had. It's easy to forget she's actually Mamma's caseworker. Actually, I guess she's responsible for our whole family. It's funny to think of it that way, though. Technically I know it's her job to come check in on us now and then, but she always feels more like an old family friend. She's been coming around almost as long as I can remember.

I was about three or four, I think, when Mamma had her incident. "Lost her head," as she likes to say. Gramma Patty said it was bound to happen. Back then Mamma was living with a friend and working two jobs and trying to take care of me at the same time. She went through a bad patch, missed some bills, got evicted, and I got put in foster care. But Mamma moved in with Gramma Patty and got herself together, and after a few months they said she could have me back on the condition that she kept living with Gramma Patty. And that's how we've been ever since. It works fine, and we've never had any more problems, but Renee still comes by every month or so just to check in and make sure everything is going smoothly.

I usually look forward to our meetings. Renee likes to talk to us each separately, so she'll pick me up and take me to a diner nearby and buy me a slice of pie while we talk. I tell her whatever is going on in my life, and she listens and sometimes gives advice. She's always been really supportive of my singing dreams, even early on when other people laughed at me. She says it's important for everyone to have people who believe in them.

Anyway, it was nice to talk to her about everything that's been going on with me lately. Mamma and Gramma Patty are too close to the situation for me to trust their reactions, Angela doesn't really believe me, and the doctor didn't seem to want to hear about it. Renee let me talk through the whole thing, and I did feel better at the end.

I told her about feeling tired and jumpy all the time, and my trouble with my voice, and losing my spot in the choir. I even told her about the weird nightmares or waking dreams or whatever they are, though I wasn't sure how to convey how scary they are when they're happening. Calling them dreams doesn't really capture it, but I'm not sure what else to say. (I didn't tell her about the feathers, because of what Angela said. I don't want her to think I'm out of my mind! I guess I'll just continue keeping that to myself for now.)

Renee listened to it all and fed me pie and sympathized with how awful it must be. That helped, but I still kept worrying about what Angela had said, and whether there's a truth in it that I don't want to face. It's hard not to wonder if the problems I'm having might just be in my head, but, well, if they're in my head, does that mean I really am crazy? It's scary to think I might not be able to control my own mind. And I don't *feel* crazy. Then again, maybe crazy people never do, and you just keep screaming about how sane you are as they tie you up in a straitjacket and dump you into a padded cell.

These are the kinds of things I've been thinking as I try to fall asleep at night. And let me tell you, none of it was very comforting. So I just focused on not thinking these things, not acknowledging them, and I hoped that would make them go away. I don't know why I thought that would work. I bet that's never worked in the history of humanity.

So I was a bit nervous when Renee came over today because, as much as I love her, she has this intense ability to see right through people. Or to see right through me, anyway. I guess that's part of her job. She has an uncanny sense about these things. And sure enough, much as I'd tried to hide these fears even from myself, Renee seemed to grasp them right away and give them voice. Only, when she talked about them, they didn't sound as bad as they had in my imagination. In fact, it was kind of a relief to hear her express my situation so calmly and matter-of-fact, as if these dreams were a totally normal part of life.

Basically, she listened to me whine and complain about everything that's been going badly in my life, especially about my throat and what could be wrong with it, and she just said, "Do you think it might just be stress?" And when I got nervous and tongue-tied, she put a hand over mine and said, "Laetitia, it's nothing to be ashamed of." Which I think I really needed to hear.

She talked about the relationship between the mind and the body, and how it's totally normal for mental concerns to manifest themselves in physical ways. For example, she told me that when she worked her first job after college, she had a boss who made her feel really bad about herself, and she started getting stomachaches every day. They were bad, and she was getting really worried. She thought she must have an allergy or an ulcer, or something even worse. But the day she quit her job, she had her last stomachache, and she's never had them come back since then. She said it wasn't true that it was "all in her head"—it's more that the head and the body are connected. And that it's a myth that just because something is going on in our heads, that means we should have complete control over it. You can't will yourself to get over anxiety or depression or even just a simple case of nerves any more than you can get rid of measles or the flu through pure force of will. Which I guess does make sense.

I wonder if losing my voice and getting these weird pains and visions might just be my body's way of dealing with my nerves and anxieties about the upcoming audition. It does make me feel a lot better to think that this kind of thing is pretty normal and happens to a lot of people. Renee says loads of famous professional singers have found they can't croak out a note when faced with a concert or audition that's really important to them. But while it does make me feel better that I'm not necessarily crazy, it doesn't fix the problem. Just as Renee said, knowing it's in my head doesn't make it go away. So how do I get rid of this mental block before my audition?

Renee said there was no guaranteed cure, but she did have some suggestions. She told me to spend some time in the auditorium without even trying to sing, just to get used to being back there without stressing out. We also talked about ways I could get back to singing without putting so much pressure on myself, like singing a lullaby to one of the neighborhood kids, or just singing along with the radio. Situations where I know I'm not going to be judged, and I can take pleasure in the act itself.

Then she said something that kind of caught me off guard at first, though I am trying to consider it seriously. She asked me, just as an experiment, to try picturing my future as something other than a singer. As soon as she said that, I felt myself get really upset.

I've just had this unshakeable vision of myself as a singer for so long that anything else I could conjure up felt like failure. Worse than that, it felt like a betrayal of everything I've believed in and worked for. The first images in my head were picturing myself working at a factory or a casino just to make ends meet, like my mamma. Day after day of doing something boring and pointless, with no hope of anything ever improving. Honestly, it sounded like hell. But Renee wouldn't let me leave it at that. She pushed me to think about other things I'm interested in, other things I could contribute. At first I was like, *Nothing*, but when I gave it some thought, I realized I've been excited about the photos I've been taking recently. And I love spending time working on my hair and makeup. I'm good at that, too. Maybe I'd like helping other people with it. I do those tutorials on my blog, and that's always fun. So maybe there are other things in life that could make me happy, even if I could never sing again.

I have to say, once I realized that, it was a huge relief. I instantly felt a lot better about everything. So maybe Renee was right, and I was putting too much pressure on myself to succeed on this one narrow path. And there're all kinds of other things out there in the world I haven't even tried. Maybe I've thrown myself so deeply into this one thing, assuming it's what I was always meant to do, that I've missed out on other stuff I might be just as good at, or find interesting, at least.

We talked about the Dwayne Robinson trial a bit. I guess Renee's been following it pretty closely, and she was surprised I haven't been. She says the whole country is talking about it, and it all happened just a few blocks from me! I really have let myself be pretty blind to stuff that's going on around me. I guess that's another example of something I can think about to take my mind off singing, though it might make me feel more bad than good. But it does seem to give Malcolm a sense of purpose. Maybe it can do the same for me?

It does feel a little ironic. The point of this exercise was to get me relaxed enough about singing so I'd be able to do it again, but if I wind up thinking of all this other stuff that interests me, maybe I won't even want to sing anymore. Does that mean the exercise failed? Or does that count as a success? I don't know. I still have pretty mixed feelings about it, I guess. I don't want to give up my dream, and I still feel like if you want something, you have to be single-minded and focused to get it. That's always worked for me in the past. But it's not working right now. At the same time, I'm starting to realize how self-centered my pursuit of fame and success has made me. There are so many bigger problems in

86

the world than my getting a little hoarse now and then. But does that realization become less significant if I'm only using it to help me get my voice back? It seems dishonest, somehow. Insincere.

TUESDAY, FEBRUARY 18, 4:15 P.M. (PRIVATE)

I thought maybe things were getting better after my talk with Renee, but something happened at school today. I had another one of my . . . attacks. I don't know what else to call them. It was at lunch, sitting at my usual table with a couple of friends who were talking about a movie they were thinking of going to. I was only half paying attention and was staring out the window, not really thinking about anything. That's when I felt it coming on. I guess it's happened enough times now that I know the feeling. The sense that I'm not where I seem to be, or maybe that *part* of me is right there, sitting at the lunch table, but some other part of me is far away, going through something totally different.

I knew it was coming this time, and I knew I wouldn't be able to stop it, so I tried to breathe deeply and just wait for whatever it was this time to come and go. I felt prickling all over my skin, as if I'd broken a sweat. The quality of the air seemed to change, and I couldn't really hear people around me anymore. Everything sounded distorted.

That was when my head was yanked backward, like someone had grabbed me by the hair. I could feel hot breath against my face, as if someone were leaning over me. Through all this I was scared, but I was trying to hold it together. Even as it happened, part of me knew I was still in the cafeteria with my friends nearby, and I didn't want to scare people or embarrass myself by making a big scene. I kept repeating, "It's just a dream; it's not real," even though that was not quite true.

That worked for a while, but then I felt something in my eyes. I couldn't see anything in front of me but empty air, and then the walls and ceiling of the lunch room, but I could feel it, like some kind of long metal spike being driven in. First one, then the other. And the nerves and muscles that keep your eyes in place, I could feel and hear them tearing as whatever invisible force it was ripped my eyeballs from their sockets.

That was when I lost it. I started screaming and grabbing at my head, alternating between trying to fight off my invisible attacker, and trying to use an arm to protect my eyes. I fell to the floor, and the rest is kind of a blur of my friends trying to help me, and one of the lunch room attendants pulling me from the room and taking me to the nurse's office. At that point I calmed down a bit, and the pain mostly faded, but I still couldn't see anything. The nurse asked what was wrong with me. Had someone hit me? Had I gotten some chemical in my eyes? Was I on drugs? But I couldn't give her a good answer.

She looked into my eyes with a little light, but she said they looked fine. I still couldn't see, though. At this point I was convinced I'd never see again, but I wasn't even that worried about it. I was just so exhausted by what I'd gone through and how real it felt. And that sense that I had done something terrible, and was being punished for some crime I didn't remember. I could hardly be bothered to worry about my sight.

The nurse took me into a little room and had me lie on a cot there in the dark for a while. She said I needed to calm down, and she'd check on me in an hour. Sure enough, when she turned the light back on, I could see again. It was the strangest thing.

Well, I guess I'm about ready to post this now. I'm delaying a little because I'm afraid of the ghost who lives in my computer. Or not a ghost, but I'm not sure what else to call it. Whatever it is that posts those photos whenever I write something like this. I actually thought about not writing it at all, wondering if that would keep the photo from showing up, but it didn't feel right. It's like I *need* to write it out, or else the whole thing is just in my head, and that's even worse. And to be perfectly honest, I guess I'm a little curious what the picture will be. I'm scared to look, but at the same time, I'm excited.

TUESDAY, FEBRUARY 18, 2:06 P.M. (PRIVATE)

TUESDAY, FEBRUARY 18, 4:20 P.M. (PRIVATE)

There it is, just like I was expecting. Only I think this one might
be even creepier than the others. What the hell?

Where did it come from? It's obviously not me in the picture, so who is it? Is it even a real person, or is it just something
made up out of my imagination?

The good news is it posted privately this time, instead of
popping up for anyone to see. Not that I suppose it matters anymore. As far as anyone can tell, this blog has been completely
abandoned. I suppose I should feel bad about that, but I can't
find it in me to care right now.

angela: hey. you there?

laetitia: yeah.

angela: how are you doing? are you singing again?

laetitia: not really.

angela: oh. well . . . you said on the phone before that you have trouble following my stories because my friends are just names to you. so . . . i took some pics of everyone! wanna see?

laetitia: sure, go ahead.

angela: this is tre, of course. isn't he cute??

[photo redacted]

angela: and tasha

[photo redacted]

angela: and lisa.

[photo redacted]

angela: lisa's kind of got a bit of your style, with the blue and green extensions.

laetitia: wow, yeah, tell her i love her hair.

angela: what about you? are you still keeping up your divanation these days?

laetitia: yeah, most days. did you ever see the wig i got for my birthday?

angela: um . . . idk, which is it? the blue and silver?

laetitia: no, hold on. i'm wearing it now. i'll do a selfie.

 [photo redacted]

angela: wtf is that?

laetitia: omg, i didn't mean to send that. that's not the picture.

angela: no shit! what the hell is it?

laetitia: i don't know. i've never seen it before.

angela: what the hell, laetitia? is this some kind of joke? because it's not funny!

laetitia: i told you: it's not mine. it's some kind of bug in my computer; it does this sometimes.

angela: stop lying. you know you sent it. you're sick—you know that?

angela: you've been pissing me off something fierce lately, and i tried to be cool about it because we've been friends for so long, but i am sick of your shit.

angela: you are a drama queen, and you've always got to make everything all about you. you didn't even ask me what happened with tre and his ex-girlfriend, even though i told you i was upset. i try to include you, but you couldn't care less what's going on in my life.

laetitia: what? that's not fair! there's something seriously wrong with me, and i'm supposed to care about your stupid boyfriend? my life is falling apart, i don't know what's the matter with me, and i might be losing my mind. so sorry if i can't find any room to care about you and your stupid new friends.

angela: you always do this! you always have to be the center of attention, since we were kids. you can't stand it when anything is going on in anyone else's life. and if there's nothing going on in yours, you've got no problem making stuff up until everyone acts like you're special.

laetitia: that's not true! i never do that. i'd give anything to go back to normal.

angela: forget it, laetitia. find someone else to tell your stories to. i'm done.

angela has logged off.

THURSDAY, FEBRUARY 20, 1:10 A.M. (PRIVATE)

Two different teachers came up to me today to ask if I'm okay. And I can tell some of my friends are worried about me too. I guess I must look pretty rough these days, even though I'm trying to hold it together. I wind up shrugging off my friends, because I don't know what to tell them. Anything close to the truth, and they'll just think I'm lying or crazy, like Angela does. The best I can do is keep it to myself and try to think about other stuff.

I've been reading a lot about the Dwayne Robinson trial. It's the only thing that works as a distraction from my own weird problems. I've been sitting here for three hours, reloading the same news sites in hopes of updates, and following the randomest links to see what some blogger in Spain or whoever thinks about the whole thing. Pretty weird, when I'm right *here*.

But there isn't much in the way of news. The trial is closed to the press, so everything is just speculation until the jury comes back with a verdict. But in the meantime, people have been protesting outside the courthouse. It's surreal. I can read all about this stuff online, but if I listen carefully enough, I can hear it out the windows, too. The courthouse is only a couple of miles from here. Sometimes I even see the news vans coming and going, and some people I know from school have made signs and gone down to demonstrate. I know Malcolm is one of them.

I wonder if I should go too. It would be a way of hanging out with Malcolm more, but it's not really about that, honestly. I don't really know Malcolm well, but the protests . . . I don't know. I'm curious. Interested. I guess I want to feel like I'm part of this. Like I'm contributing something.

Gramma Patty is against it, though. She says I should stay out of it. She says all the demonstrating is just getting people riled up and isn't helping anything at all. I guess that's what the pastor has been saying too: there's nothing for any of us to do at this point but wait and hope for justice to be served. Honestly, I don't see how it can fail. That video is *so* clear. Still, I wish I didn't feel so helpless. It's awful to sit here, clicking through page after page, looking for any new information, even when I know it can't help. But then again, if I could really help, if there was something I should be doing, I guess that would be a lot of pressure too. So I don't know which way to feel.

Gramma Patty's afraid there will be riots if the policemen get off, and the whole city will burn. Mamma's nervous too, I can tell, but she shows it in different ways. Instead of just responding directly to whatever's on the news, Mamma's got feelings that "come over her," or "little episodes" where her eyelids flutter and she has to press a hand to her chest for a few seconds. Gramma Patty rolls her eyes at these and mutters about Mamma being such a drama queen. But Mamma's emotions manifest in different ways from most people, so she's not sleeping well and wakes up at the drop of a hat (which I notice, since I haven't been sleeping well lately either).

Every night she has a new story. She's hearing doors banging and dogs barking and voices whispering in her ear. The other night she made a huge drama just because the light in the bathroom kept flickering. She kept saying it was a sign or something. A sign of what? Probably that the bulb needs to be replaced, if you ask me. But Mamma's always been a bit like this—excitable, I guess you'd say. All the stuff the pastor talks about with angels and devils and spirits and whatnot, Mamma doesn't always leave that stuff in church, where it belongs. Especially when she gets jumpy about something and isn't sleeping well. I get the feeling that sometimes she's a little unclear on the line between her dreams and reality. But then, I guess I shouldn't talk. These days, I'm not much better.

THURSDAY, FEBRUARY 20, 6:38 A.M. (PRIVATE)

Holy Jesus, I did not need that this morning! *Gross.*

I was getting ready for school and I just went to put on my wig—it's one of my favorites, kind of a shimmery lavender color. I wore it just last week and put it away on its stand like I always do. And this morning I'm brushing it out and getting it ready to set in place, and I notice something flutter to the ground. So I lean over to check it out, and it's a *moth*. How the hell did a moth get into my wig? I've never heard of that before. Ew, this is something that sits on my *head*.

Of course the first thing I did was yelp and sweep it away from me with my hand, and it flew into a corner. But now it's just sitting there in that corner, which doesn't really solve anything. I guess I'm going to have to get a tissue so I can pick it up and throw it away.

THURSDAY, FEBRUARY 20, 6:46 A.M. (PRIVATE)

I was going to just toss the stupid moth outside or flush it down the toilet, but before I did, I opened the tissue to peek at it, because if something has been hanging out in my hair, I should at least know what it looks like, right? It was kind of pretty, actually. Not like a beautiful butterfly or anything, but where I had expected to be horrified by this dead thing, I was fascinated instead.

For some reason, I couldn't bring myself to just toss it away. I don't know why, but I didn't want it to be like it had never happened. I wanted to document it somehow. Then I remembered my dead animal pics that Gramma Patty didn't like, and I figured, why not add to my collection? So I took a photo and now I guess I'll post it. It should fit right in with the stuff I've been posting lately.

Sometimes I can't help imagining what my old followers would think if they could see my blog now, if I ever made all these posts public. I bet they'd be so scandalized, to see that their source for hair tutorials has morphed into dead bugs and mold. Of course, maybe if I'd stayed public, I would have wound up with a new kind of follower. There's got to be someone out there who appreciates this type of stuff.

But for now I'd rather just keep it for me.

Thursday, February 20, 10:35 P.M. (Private)

Something is definitely not okay. Finding that moth in my wig this morning freaked me out a little, but it seemed like just a fluke thing. What's one little moth? I didn't see any damage, and I checked my other wigs and everything looked okay. So I picked a different one—the red and black—and I styled it and wore it to school and it was fine. I put the whole thing out of my mind. Except tonight I was getting ready for bed and I go to take it off, and a handful of little moths fall to the floor, *ew*.

It must be some kind of infestation. I hate to say it, but I think I'm going to stay away from my wigs for a little while until I figure out what's going on. I'll just do turbans and wraps for a few days.

It's not the wigs. It can't be. But if it isn't, I don't even want to think about what's going on.

All I know is I was having one of those nightmares last night. There isn't really any story to them, just the scenes I've been through before, repeating themselves on a loop—the torture, the pain of the wheel, the grill, the arrows, the spike prying out my eyes, and the terrible sense I've done something to deserve it but can't remember what. Then I woke up into darkness, feeling kind of dizzy and disoriented. So I just lay there for a few minutes, until I noticed this weird tickling feeling in my ear. I reached up to scratch at it, and there was something *there*. Under my fingernail. Something that wasn't my skin. And instantly all I could think was, *Get it out get it out get it out*. So I sat up and sort of flicked my finger into my ear, and this big ass moth falls into my lap. Like, at least an inch big! I screamed so loud then, I woke the whole house up.

By the time Mamma got to my room, I was totally freaked out. I swear, it felt like the moth had squirmed out from inside of me.

Gramma Patty tried to calm me down. She said it didn't come from inside my ear; it must have flown around the room and landed on me in the night. I don't know, though. Her explanation does make more sense than mine, but somehow I still *felt* it coming out of me. Maybe I got mixed up by that dream I was having.

FRIDAY, FEBRUARY 21, 6:15 A.M. (PRIVATE)

I spent the rest of last night in the living room, with the TV going and all the lights on. I knew if I got back into bed, I would spend the whole night feeling powdery little wings brushing against my skin until I drove myself crazy. But that meant this morning I went back into the room to get dressed and saw the big moth just lying there on the floor, where I must have knocked it to the ground. I wonder how it died. . . . It was definitely alive in my ear last night. Did I give it a heart attack or something? Can moths die of shock? But it was not moving at all, so it's definitely dead now.

I moved it to a sunny spot and took a picture. I don't know why it makes me feel better to do that, but it does. I think it's the process of it that calms me down. When I sit here, thinking, *Gross bugs are crawling on me in my sleep,* of course that freaks me out, and all I want to do is scream and scream, but if I can force myself to think, *This would make an interesting photo*, it changes my whole relationship to the situation. Instead of screaming, *Get it off me, get it off me!*, I have to pick it up with my own hands and put it down somewhere, and then I have to position it and move it around to capture it at the best angle. I know this is weird, but at some point it starts to feel almost like a gift. That someone gave me this strange, beautiful thing, and it's my job to honor it the only way I know how. It almost feels like it's part of me, and I can't just cast it off until I've documented it in some way. It would be like throwing away a piece of my own self, or my experience, anyway.

So I take the picture. Then I can take the thing outside and feel much calmer about it.

Gramma Patty caught me doing all this and made me let her feel my head, as if she thought I were running a fever. I felt okay, but she still looked worried. I think at this point, it's my mental health she is worrying about more than physical, but Mamma says it is a good instinct to document everything that is going on, so we can show people if we need to. I don't know who in their right mind would want to know any of this, but it keeps Gramma Patty off my back at least.

FRIDAY, FEBRUARY 21, 9:29 A.M. (PRIVATE)

Mamma let me stay home from school today because of the fright I had last night. I still can't explain it, but it definitely kept me from sleeping well the rest of the night. This morning I was a complete zombie, so Mamma told me to stay home and get some rest, and maybe I'd be able to go in for my afternoon classes. That sounded like a good idea, except now I *still* can't sleep. Every time I close my eyes, I can feel that moth flapping around on me, that tickling sensation in my ear that makes my skin crawl, and I wake myself up, trying to scratch these imaginary insects off my body. I might as well have gone into school, since it's not like I'm getting any rest. But I really don't think I would have been able to focus on my classes. All I can really handle right now is sitting here on the couch, wrapped in a blanket, watching TV and messing around on my laptop.

I feel a little guilty about that. Gramma Patty and Mamma have both been trying to get me to stay away from the coverage of the Robinson trial because they're convinced that's what's upsetting me and giving me bad dreams. Gramma Patty in particular always makes me shut off the news if she catches me looking at it. She says it's not healthy. That it's making us all edgy, and there's nothing we can do anyway. I get what she's saying, but even though it's frustrating to feel so powerless, somehow I can't look away. It's like I'm obsessed.

I've never taken much interest in the news before, but this doesn't just feel like any old dry news story. Maybe because it's so close. The whole world is talking about it, but it all happened right here, so it feels, in a small way, like it's about us. It makes my voice problems and feeling sick all the time, and Mamma being weird about nighttime noises seem like less of a big deal when I see Robinson's father crying on TV and his cousins talking about the unfairness of it all.

Sometimes I wonder if maybe it's wrong of me to get comfort, or at least distraction, from another family's misery. To use them as an excuse to get out of my own skin a little and worry about someone else's problems. Maybe this has nothing to do with me. Maybe I'm just rubbernecking, like Gramma Patty says. But she and Mamma are both out of the house now, so I am taking this opportunity to feed my addiction.

That sounds kind of weird, doesn't it? Am I addicted to watching stuff about the trial? Usually when people talk about addiction, it has to do with pointless and destructive pleasures, like drugs or drinking or gambling. Can it really be considered an addiction to take an interest in current events? It's not destructive. But then, if it's keeping me awake at night, or getting me upset, is that destructive? Is it pointless? Or is it worse to close your eyes to the bad things in the world, so you can enjoy your own bit of peace? I don't know, but it is true that I feel a little sneaky, using this day off from school to indulge my obsession instead of trying to get some rest, like I'm supposed to.

FRIDAY, FEBRUARY 21, 10:52 A.M. (PRIVATE)

My throat feels really weird.

I was just sitting here on the couch, watching the news station and flipping around to get the latest stories about the Robinson case. They were talking about Robinson, but it almost felt like watching a documentary of my life. I recognize the street he grew up on and the playgrounds where he played. The street corner where he was shot is one I pass at least once a week. It all feels very close, in a way that is both scary and impossible to look away from.

Anyway, I was feeling drowsy and I must have fallen asleep at some point, because the next thing I knew, I was startled out of another nightmare.

It started out just like the others I've been having, where I'm forced to revisit all these horrible scenes of torture—burned alive, pierced with arrows, strapped to a giant wheel, eyes ripped out. Then the scene shifted, and I was caught in a fire. I think my dream must have gotten mixed up with a story on the news. I could feel the searing heat and hear the crackling of the flames mixed with the sound of distant sirens and the smell of burning flesh. My skin felt like it was prickling and crawling, but when I looked down, expecting to see flames licking up my body, instead I was covered in a blanket of different-colored moths, each beating its papery wings against my skin. And I couldn't tell which was hallucinated, the fire or the moths, and whether the creepy, crawly feeling was from thousands of fluttering wings or from my skin curling off as it burned.

I woke myself up, coughing, even though there wasn't any smoke in the house. Actually, I'd been coughing all morning and thought I was coming down with a cold, or that I wasn't all the way better from the one I'd had before, but it's worse now.

I just had to stop writing to deal with another big coughing fit. But no matter how much I cough, it doesn't seem to give me any relief. It doesn't quite feel like the usual tickle in the throat or something. It feels more like there is something solid and heavy lodged in my esophagus or my windpipe, I can't tell which. I keep pressing on it from the outside, but I'm not sure if I can really feel anything or if I'm just imagining it. I keep wanting to cough and hack and retch just to bring it up, but I'm also a little afraid of the massive phlegm ball I'm going to produce if I do ever manage to bring it up. I wish it would just go away on its own, but it's probably healthier if I keep coughing. Better out than in?

I just looked in my hand mirror, and my throat was a little hard to see from the angle, but I think I can actually see something under the skin of my neck, like it's swollen or something. And there are some weird shapes, but I'm not sure what my throat usually looks like. Maybe it's just swollen glands and I am freaking myself out over nothing. I'm going to take some more cough medicine, I think.

What the holy hell just came out of me? I don't understand. It doesn't make any sense. How is it possible that my body produced that?

I know what it is, even though I don't think I've ever seen one up close before. It's a seashell. And I live about a thousand miles from the coast. How in the hell . . . ? Jesus help me; I know this isn't right.

FRIDAY, FEBRUARY 21, 11:26 A.M. (PRIVATE)

Okay. I'm calmer now. But look at that thing. It's huge. I'm trying so hard to think of any reasonable explanation for how I could have coughed this up, but I've got nothing.

God, what is wrong with me? I just searched the whole Internet and freaked myself out with all the stories of horrible parasites people have picked up on vacation, plus a lot of stuff about people who ate some bad clams and got food poisoning, but nothing like this. What is happening? When is it going to stop?

I know Mamma is still at work for a few hours, but I have to call her.

FRIDAY, FEBRUARY 21, 2:19 P.M. (PRIVATE)

I'm at the clinic now, waiting to be seen by Dr. Afolabi. I know I was nervous about telling the doctor this stuff before, but it's gone too far. I can't just keep ignoring this.

Mamma came straight home from work when I told her what had happened. I hope she doesn't get in trouble for that. Her supervisor isn't always very sympathetic about family problems, and Mamma's been trying to cut down on her "emergencies," I know, but what else was I supposed to do?

Mamma came home to check on me, and she called the doctor's office and was trying to set up an appointment sometime in the next few days. And right then and there, with Mamma on the phone, I got that feeling again. She turned around when she heard me start to cough and choke, and got me a glass of water and whacked me on the back a few times. But I knew by then what was happening. The only question was what I would bring up this time. Finally it came loose, and I spat up a mess of bile and blood and small bones, like from an animal. I just sat there for a while, shivering and staring at the mess I had made, only vaguely conscious of Mamma telling the receptionist there had been a change of plans, and we needed to see the doctor immediately.

Then she wrapped the shell and the bones up in a little sandwich baggie to bring with us, and she called a taxi to take us to the clinic, which we *never* do. I can't remember the last time we had an emergency that couldn't wait for the bus.

But for all that rush, we still had to wait for the doctor, so that's why I'm updating on my phone right now. Moths, shells, bones . . . and the feathers . . . What's the connection? I hope someone will be able to help me figure it out.

FRIDAY, FEBRUARY 21, 3:38 P.M. (PRIVATE)

Just got out of the clinic, on the bus home now. I met with Dr. Afolabi, but I don't know what good it did, or even if she understands the problem.

She started by checking me over as usual, and shining a light in my throat and ears and nose. Then she asked me a bunch of questions. Am I eating or drinking anything different? Any change in routine? She started off with these sort of normal, harmless questions, but then at some point she stopped and said, "You know you can tell me anything and I can't tell your mother or anyone else. It's a rule: I can't tell them no matter what you tell me."

I told her I understood, so she was like, "Is there anything else you want to tell me? Anything else going on in your life?"

That confused me. Is there likely to be something more sig-

telling the truth. Why would I lie? I was getting enough attention without any of this. This isn't the kind of attention I ever wanted.

Mamma sat down at the table, looking exhausted and put out and worried all at the same time. She told me the doctor said sometimes people make this stuff up—especially teenagers—because there are some other problems going on in their lives that they can't talk about for some reason, but they need people to notice them. And people aren't noticing the real problem, so they try to make themselves noticed for other stuff. I asked her what would count as a "real" problem, and she said violence, like abuse. Or other stuff. And then she looked at me with big eyes and made me promise to tell her if anything was going on, if anyone was touching me how they shouldn't be, or anything at all, and I shouldn't feel afraid to tell her. So I was like, "I'm not! I wouldn't be." But there isn't anything like that. I don't know how to make anyone believe me. It isn't that. It's something else.

Mamma hugged me and said that was what she told the doctor. That she was the crazy one, not me. I hope that's true.

The point is that Mamma does believe me, even if the doctor doesn't. That's the important thing. But it doesn't solve the problem. The truth is, I never really believed the doctor would help anyway. I hoped she would, but if I'm honest with myself, I have to accept that this doesn't seem to be a medical problem. I can't think of any normal disease that makes you cough up animal parts.

nificant on my mind than the fact that I am gagging up bizarre objects? So I said no, pretty much just the puking thing. But she kept asking, so I mentioned how I've been having bad dreams, and that I lost my singing voice. She seemed a little interested in that, but she kept digging for something else. I don't know what. And then she asked me all these questions about self-harm—have I ever cut or burned or scratched myself on purpose? Do I restrict calories or exercise excessively or use laxatives? Have I become sexually active? All this health class stuff that didn't seem to have anything to do with anything.

Of course I told her no to all that stuff, and eventually she let me go, but then she told me to send Mamma back in without me. So I just sat in the waiting room, playing with my phone, and when Mamma came out, she had such a look on her face! She was *pissed*, and I don't know what the doctor must have said to her. She wouldn't even talk to me; she just grabbed me by the arm and steered me out to the bus stop, and she was fuming and muttering under her breath the whole time. I'm starting to get really nervous that the doctor said something bad about me and I'm about to get in huge trouble. Only I can't imagine what it might be. I really don't think I did anything wrong. All I can make out from her muttering is something about "calling my daughter a liar" and "Who does she think she is?" and such. I don't know what that's about, and Mamma doesn't seem inclined to discuss it on public transportation. I guess I'll find out more when we get home.

FRIDAY, FEBRUARY 21, 4:08 P.M. (PRIVATE)

Well, now I know what Dr. Afolabi was thinking, I guess. And why Mamma was so mad about it.

The moment we got home, Mamma practically hauled me into the living room and sat me down on the couch so she could pace in front of me, and she started babbling away about how that doctor is a quack and doesn't know what she is doing and we are never going to her again. So I asked what happened, what did she say, what's going on with me? I was still convinced Dr. Afolabi told her I had some kind of terrible disease or something, or I've done something awful without even realizing it, because Mamma looked so upset, but I wanted to know, whatever it was, because at least that would be an answer.

So I was practically begging her to just spit it out, and Mamma grabbed my arm again, tight, and said, "What you told me about those things you coughed up—was that the truth? I mean the real honest-to-God truth?" So I told her, "Yeah, of course it is." But that wasn't enough for her, and she kept asking me the same basic question in a bunch of different ways unti I was crying as I tried to defend myself, and I didn't even know what I was being accused of. But I guess finally I convinced he because at last she let go of me and nodded and then muttere "Stupid doctor. I ought to have her license."

I still didn't understand what the doctor had said that h gotten Mamma so upset, so she explained that Dr. Afolabi called me a liar. She said I had just found a shell and some b somewhere and made up this whole story to get Mamm come home from work. I was so shocked! Why would I do I've never been so willful or troublesome in my whole life the doctor said I might be faking everything to get attenti

I didn't know what to say. How could I possibly be fak Mamma saw me cough up those bones. And Mamma sa told the doctor that. Told her she saw it with her own ey the doctor said that kind of thing is easy to fake. That it l all the time. Kids hide stuff in their cheeks, their hand sleeves. Like a magician palming a card. You can hid until the last minute and then make it look like you them up.

I asked Mamma if she believed Dr. Afolabi, and said, "No, of course not." She said she told that doctor lie to her. That I had never lied to her.

I felt a little guilty when she said that. Why did s put it like that? It's not like I've *never* lied to Mar kid in the history of the Earth has gotten through without ever telling a lie? But this time, *this* time, I

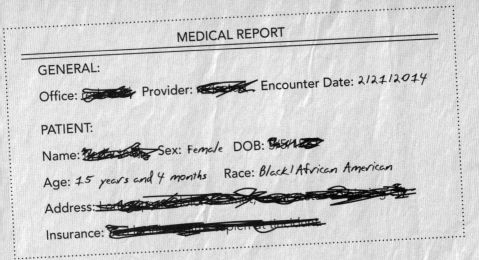

GENERAL:

Office: ~~████~~ Provider: ~~████~~ Encounter Date: 2/27/2074

PATIENT:

Name: ~~████~~ Sex: Female DOB: ~~████~~

Age: 15 years and 4 months Race: Black/African American

Address: ~~████~~

Insurance: ~~████~~

COMPLAINT:

Patient complains of intense vomiting sessions resulting in the disgorgement of odd (nonedible) objects. Patient's mother brought in and presented the objects (seashell and small animal bones) supposedly disgorged by the patient. Patient also suffers from the loss of her voice, which presented seven weeks ago. Patient claims only her singing voice is affected. Speaking voice appears normal.

EXAMINATION:

No organic causes for symptoms revealed during physical examination. Throat appears slightly inflamed. Throat cultures returned negative. No tests run on the objects presented by patient's mother at this time.

DIAGNOSIS:

Diagnosis is undetermined at this time, but symptoms strongly indicate an underlying psychological issue. Further examination by a psychiatrist is recommended. Symptoms are typical of adolescents with past or ongoing traumatic experiences, but the patient shut down all inquiries into possible sources of trauma in her life. Strong possibility of physical, sexual, or psychological abuse, most likely on the part of someone close to the patient, whom the patient feels compelled to protect. Alternatively, a diagnosis of histrionic personality disorder or borderline personality disorder may be indicated. Recommendation: contact social services caseworker ~~████████~~.

SATURDAY, FEBRUARY 22, 2:18 A.M. (PRIVATE)

I can't sleep. I've been turning it over and over in my head. What if that doctor is right? Is it possible this stuff is all in my head? I mean, it feels so real, but the mind can work in strange ways. I don't *think* I've experienced any kind of sexual abuse, or other form of abuse, or any other deep dark secret, but how can I be sure? How can you ever be sure of the secrets you hide from your own self?

The doctor said if it wasn't trauma-related, it could be a symptom of another problem. Mental illness. Is that it? I mean, it's not like I hadn't considered the possibility before, but it's different when a doctor is saying it. That makes it feel more real. Sometimes it *does* feel like I'm going crazy. Like I don't even recognize myself. But the idea that I can't trust my own sense, my reactions, my memories and experiences—it's too terrifying to even think about.

SATURDAY, FEBRUARY 22, 3:12 A.M. (PRIVATE)

Mamma heard me tossing and turning, and came in to check on me. I told her about all my worries, and she helped calm me down. She doesn't think I'm crazy. Even if I can't judge myself from the inside, she should be able to tell, right?

Mamma says there is something going on with me, but it's the kind of thing doctors don't understand. For this kind of illness, only God can fix it. She says someone must have hexed us or put the evil eye on us, and that we need to call on a higher power for protection. Normally I roll my eyes when Mamma talks this way. She's also convinced God is the answer to a *lot* of life's questions. I've never taken it all too seriously, but in the middle of the night, when I was feeling so scared and anxious, I have to admit it did feel comforting—the idea of putting this problem in God's hands and letting Him take care of it.

Why shouldn't it work? Whether the problem is medical or mental or who knows what else, it all comes from God in the first place. So whatever it is, it's in His power to fix it. Or if not, I don't see how it can hurt, at least.

SATURDAY, FEBRUARY 22, 9:22 A.M. (PRIVATE)

When I came down to breakfast this morning, Mamma had a glint in her eye like she had just thought up the most marvelous thing. Sure enough, before I could even pour some cereal, she grabbed me by the hand and made us all stand in a circle in the middle of the kitchen while she said a blessing. She does some kind of blessing or prayer every morning, but this was more than her usual bit about the food and preparing for a good day. She took her time and talked about evil forces that had invaded the household, and asked for God's protection from them. Then she squeezed my hand extra hard as we said our amens.

So I guess that was her plan. I did feel better while she was doing it, so who knows? Maybe it will help. But it's hard to imagine something so simple and straightforward could make a difference, given the strange stuff I've been going through. But prayer can be pretty powerful, as Gramma Patty always tells me. We'll see, I guess.

When I got home from school today, Renee was waiting for me, even though this isn't our usual day for a meeting. Apparently, the doctor put in a call about me after my appointment the other day. She told social services I was showing signs of abuse, and that she was concerned about what was going on in our household.

I don't understand it, though. The doctor told me I could tell her anything and she wasn't allowed to tell anyone. She said it was part of her job: that she's not allowed to share my secrets with anyone. So how could she then turn around and call social services and talk to who knows how many people before the message reached Renee? Renee didn't seem eager to talk about that and kept trying to change the subject, but finally she said Dr. Afolabi had to do it, and that she did the right thing by calling social services. As far as I can tell, that means all the stuff she was telling me about privacy and confidentiality was just a lie.

Renee argued with me about that. She said what the doctor told me is true, but that there are exceptions. Very specific exceptions that are designed to protect and help people. That's nice and all, but I'd like to see what Mamma and Gramma Patty would think if I told them there were "exceptions" to the truths I tell them. I don't think they'd be impressed.

Renee said sometimes making sure people are okay is more important than guarding their secrets, and that I shouldn't blame Dr. Afolabi, because she was just doing her job. She's legally required to call in anytime she sees something that might be considered evidence of child abuse. The exceptions are meant to protect the most vulnerable people, the ones who can't always speak up to help themselves.

Is that how Renee sees me? Vulnerable? Unable to speak up for myself? She says she and Dr. Afolabi are just being careful, but it seems to me like this rule was meant to help little kids, babies, or maybe people with mental problems who really can't speak for themselves because they don't even fully understand what's going on. But that's not me. I may not be an adult, but I'm not a little kid. I know what's real and what's not. I know what I've experienced. I told the doctor there was nothing abusive or anything like that going on. Why wasn't that enough?

Then again, I suppose if you're the kind of person who doesn't fully understand what's going on, you might not know it, which would be all the more reason for authorities to be extra careful with you. Does that describe me? I've heard of repressed memories and stuff. What if they're right, and I can't tell the difference between reality and fantasy anymore? What if I really don't know what's going on in my own life, or in my own head? I suppose it's good to know at least there are people out there, trying to help, though it's also frustrating to feel like I don't know who I can trust.

mortgage payments) have been managed successfully, and have not significantly affected L—. I conducted interviews with all members of the household, but could find no significant evidence of abuse or other recent trauma. L— does report unusual symptoms that may be an effort to win attention from the adults in her life. L— also has an audition coming up that she is very focused on. It seems likely that her symptoms are a result of this new stress and pressure in her life.

CONCLUSION:

No call for further action at this time, but I will stay in close contact with the ●●● family and remain alert to any further signs of abuse, disruption, or instability in the household.

I just called Renee to apologize for our argument. After thinking about it awhile, I've come around to see her point.

She asked me if I was ready to tell her what's really going on, and I didn't know what to say. I don't know what to tell her, or what she'll believe. I'm not even sure what's going on in my own head. So I just repeated the stuff I had already told her, about the nightmares and visions and vomiting strange things. I explained that that's why I'd gone to the doctor. But just like Dr. Afolabi, Renee didn't seem to want to take any of it at face value. She kept pressing to see if there was something more I wasn't saying, which was frustrating. Everyone's got their theories and I know they want to help, but in the meantime, I feel like no one is really listening to me.

Renee stressed again that I could trust her, and that she's

there to help and has always been on my side, and how important it was for me to tell her everything, and that I should call her right away if I have anything else I want to tell her. But what's the point when she just hears what she wants to hear instead of what I'm saying?

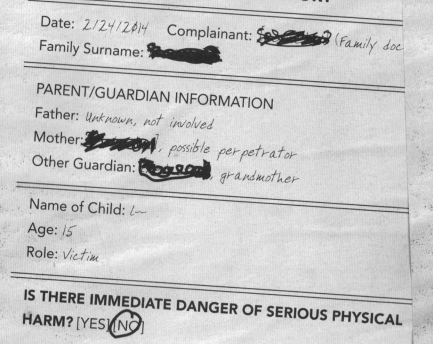

ALLEGATIONS OF CHILD ABUSE OR NEGLE
PRELIMINARY REPORT

Date: 2/24/2014   Complainant: ~~████████~~ (Family doc
Family Surname: ~~████████~~

PARENT/GUARDIAN INFORMATION
Father: Unknown, not involved
Mother: ~~████████~~, possible perpetrator
Other Guardian: ~~████████~~, grandmother

Name of Child: L—
Age: 15
Role: Victim

IS THERE IMMEDIATE DANGER OF SERIOUS PHYSICAL HARM? [YES] (NO)

ALLEGATION:
Family doctor contacted social services to report symptoms possibly indicative of abuse or other trauma affecting L—. Recommended a home welfare check.

ANALYSIS OF SITUATION:
[R. S., ~~███~~ family's regular caseworker]
On Monday, February 24, I responded to a recent alert from the ~~████~~ family's doctor, suggesting a possibility of abuse or other trauma affecting the adolescent daughter, L—. The ~~████~~ family has been fairly stable for many years now, and what few crises have arisen (work conflicts, late

TUESDAY, FEBRUARY 25, 4:45 P.M. (PRIVATE)

When I got home from school today, Mamma was very upset about something. She started in on me as soon as I walked through the door, making comments about how I'm too trusting, how you can't rely on anyone but your own family, and how other people come in here and they don't understand what's going on and they just want to make trouble.

I couldn't figure out what any of it was about, but Gramma Patty explained that while I had been at school, Renee came over again and questioned both of them on what's been going on recently, and was digging pretty hard for information. She said Renee told them that if she got any hint that this household was not a safe home for me, she would remove me, just like when I was little.

Can you believe that? Remove me! From my own home!

Like I'm a . . . dog or a bag of trash or a broken TV set. Just a thing you move from one place to another, not a person with her own choices and opinions and preferences.

This is all crazy! I told Renee a dozen times that I'm not being abused. Gramma Patty explained that it doesn't necessarily have to be abuse. I guess social services can decide to remove me if I'm not being well provided for, or if they decide the household isn't "stable" enough, whatever that means. But seriously, where does Renee get off, making these kinds of threats? After going on and on the other day about how I could trust her, and how she only wanted the best for me, how is it in my interest to take me away from my family without even consulting me?

I was furious when I realized what was going on, but Gramma Patty tried to calm me down. She said the main point is, we all have to be really cautious about what we say to Renee from now on. She agreed it would be difficult, because we've all come to trust Renee and treat her like part of the family, but we really need to be careful, because when things get rough, you can't exactly trust people from government agencies. Guess I'm learning that now.

I still can't believe it. I've always trusted Renee, and even yesterday on the phone she kept saying over and over that I could trust her, had to trust her, had to tell her anything that was going on. But Dr. Afolabi had said the same thing the other day, and it turned out she was lying. Renee said it wasn't a lie, but it smells a lot like one. And Renee is on the same side as the doctor, so of course she would protect her. But they both said they were trying to protect me and they're on my side. This whole question of "sides" is suddenly a lot less clear. I hadn't really questioned it at the time, but now that I think about it, what exactly was Renee going to do if I told her about some personal crisis? Was she going to magically wave a wand and fix it? She never said, but now it seems like her plan was always to remove me from my home and put me in foster care, just like they did when I was a baby.

I've never felt so betrayed. For years now I've told Renee all about my problems, and she's always been helpful. But those were normal problems. People teasing me at school, or a boy I was shy around, or trouble with my algebra. Renee never threatened to take me away from my family for any of that. She just talked me through whatever I was struggling with and helped me figure out a solution. But I can see this situation is different. This isn't going to be fixed by hiring a tutor or talking to a teacher.

I don't know what to do. I've trusted Renee with all my worries and concerns for so long, I don't know how to stop now. But Mamma and Gramma Patty are right. If Renee is making these kinds of threats now, based on nothing, I can't trust her anymore. But if I shut her out completely, that could go wrong too. I'm going to have to be a lot more careful from now on with who I tell what.

FRIDAY, FEBRUARY 28, 6:45 A.M. (PRIVATE)

I'm starting to worry Mamma is right about there being some kind of hex on this house. I thought she was just being her usual dramatic self, but I woke up last night to all kinds of crazy noises, like every door in the house being slammed. I guess the back door had been opened somehow, and wind was blowing all through the house. There were papers and things everywhere, and photographs had been knocked over. Then Mamma went into the kitchen and let out a scream like you wouldn't believe. There were muddy footprints on the floor. Not from shoes, but naked feet.

On one hand, maybe that's an overreaction to just footprints. But on the other, it *is* pretty creepy. Who could be walking around our house in the middle of the night with no shoes on? It wasn't me.

Gramma Patty is trying to calm her down now, but Mamma is like, "You know what this is. We can't keep denying it. It's only going to get worse. We have to do something."

I don't know what exactly she means, but it doesn't sound good. Lately Mamma and Gramma Patty have been having quiet conversations when they think I can't hear. There's something they both know that they are trying to hide from me. Maybe Mamma thinks it's more than a simple hex. Maybe it's something even worse.

But if it is what Mamma thinks, that means our prayer circle the other day didn't work. And if prayer doesn't work in a situation like this, what will?

SUNDAY, MARCH 2, 12:25 P.M. (PRIVATE)

In church this morning, Pastor Bob was talking about the Robinson trial again. On the news they're saying the verdict will be any day now, so he was talking about how people should handle the outcome, whatever it is. Everyone is still worrying about riots, and Pastor Bob went on and on about how violence only begets violence, and how this community has to focus on positive, productive steps forward. He told everyone to try to stay calm and remember to check in on their neighbors, to take care of one another. To remember there will be justice in the fullness of time, and it's not our place to be impatient and demand justice in our own time. And that rioting mostly hurts people within the community, and not the objects of everyone's anger.

I glanced around to look for Malcolm's response to that, but I guess he's stopped coming to church lately. I don't even see him at school that often. From what I hear, he's gotten so wound up in all the protesting that he doesn't have time for much else. I know Malcolm isn't in favor of rioting, but he doesn't have much patience for passive resistance, either. He says passive is exactly how they want us.

It's hard to imagine any outcome other than a guilty verdict, but I wonder what would happen if the cops were acquitted of the charges. Would all the peaceful protests and demonstrations erupt into violence? What would that look like? Would Mamma and Gramma Patty and I be in danger? Or would I get caught up in it and wind up joining the angry mob in my shock over the outcome? What if I got hurt? What if I got arrested? I've never imagined anything like that for myself before. My whole life, I've only seen one future for myself: singing on a stage in front of an adoring crowd. What if I don't live to see that destiny? What if our house gets set on fire by rioters and we all burn to death in our beds?

But maybe that's missing the point of the sermon. It does seem a little wrong to think about this situation only in terms of how it might affect me. Maybe Mamma and Gramma Patty *will* protect me. Maybe I will stay home, safe, while the riots rage, and nothing much will change in my life. But that doesn't mean stuff won't change for other people. What does it matter if I am safe and well taken care of and basically unaffected if other people just like me are being hauled off to jail or shot with rubber bullets or teargassed? Or if their homes and businesses are destroyed, their schools closed, the roads blocked off?

After the service, I just wanted to go home and think about all this stuff, but Mamma insisted on us sticking around for the doughnut hour, which I usually try to avoid. Mamma grabbed me by the arm and tugged me over to a heavyset woman wearing a coral-pink suit and a nice double string of pearls.

Mamma introduced her as Miss Nephtalie Pierre. I know I've seen her around church before. She and Mamma catch up a few times a year during the doughnut hour, but Gramma Patty is always a bit standoffish with her. And Gramma Patty isn't the only one. Miss Pierre certainly has her friends and acquaintances at church, but there are also a lot of people who seem to avoid her, don't speak to her, or even meet her eyes. It's weird, because you never saw a more respectable-looking woman. She's always nicely dressed in pastel-colored suits and a double string of pearls. She has a pleasant face and a warm, welcoming manner, and I can't think why anyone would avoid her.

Miss Pierre brushed some powdered sugar from her suit and gave us both a big smile. She asked about Mamma's health, and then turned to me and said, "And my, how you've grown!" It was odd, because I wasn't sure we'd ever directly met before, but I guess she must have known me when I was a little kid, which makes it even stranger that Mamma has barely spoken to her since then, though they seem friendly enough.

Mamma surprised me by asking if Miss Pierre would come by the house sometime this week, even though we pretty much never have people over. Then she leaned in and added in a whisper that she understood Miss Pierre was busy, but the situation was urgent. Miss Pierre dropped her smile at that point. She just nodded and pulled a little book from her purse, made a mark with her pencil, and said, "Tuesday evening." Then she said, "Do you remember what you need to do to prepare? Or do you need instructions?" Mamma said she remembered, and grabbed Miss

Pierre's hand to thank her. Then we collected Gramma Patty and went home.

How mysterious! What could this all be about? I tried to interrogate Mamma on the walk home, but she just said Miss Pierre was going to help us take care of whatever was going on. "Don't worry," she said. "She knows what she's doing; she'll fix it right up." I wanted to ask more questions, but Gramma Patty was still frowning about the whole thing, so I thought I'd better just leave it alone. I guess I won't have long to wait to find out more.

SUNDAY, MARCH 2, 3:15 P.M. (PRIVATE)

All I want to do is spend my Sunday afternoon relaxing and maybe catching up on whatever is going on with the Robinson trial to see if there are new analyses out with a different take on the situation, but Mamma is driving me crazy, cleaning everything inside and out in preparation for Miss Pierre's visit! I still don't understand exactly who she is or why she's coming over, but I have never seen Mamma clean like this. Normally she leaves all that stuff to Gramma Patty, but this time Gramma Patty just sat on the couch, watching TV while Mamma scrubbed everything down with bleach and water. I don't think it's such a good idea, to be honest. Bleach is one thing in the bathroom, but it's leaving ugly marks through the rest of the house. It makes the whole place smell funny, and the fumes make me light-headed. I don't know what Mamma thinks she's doing, but she just told me either I can help or I can stay out of the way.

I just heard Mamma and Gramma Patty talking quietly in the front room, like they didn't want me to hear. Gramma Patty was saying, "You know I think this is a bad idea. This is not how I raised you. This is not faith; it's superstition, and it betrays a lack of faith in God." To which Mamma said, "It would be more irresponsible at this point not to try it. You can't keep pretending this isn't happening." Then she went on about how there's no shame in using whatever tools are at our disposal, and that it worked last time. She specifically said, "You can't deny that it worked last time."

Last time? When? What are they talking about? Now I'm more curious than ever.

SUNDAY, MARCH 2, 3:35 P.M. (PRIVATE)

Mamma kicked me out of my own room to scrub it down! She told me to just leave her to it, but it was driving me crazy, imagining her splashing caustic chemicals all over my stuff. I went into the kitchen for a minute, and when I came back, she was holding one of my wigs in her hand, the bucket of bleach at her feet. I took the wig back and said, "Don't even think about it." There are limits.

What is all this about? It's like she's lost her mind.

MONDAY, MARCH 3, 8:36 P.M. (PRIVATE)

The tension's been building between Mamma and Gramma
Patty ever since church yesterday, and I knew they'd wind up
having it out. I'm not even sure who started it, but I was just
ducking into the kitchen to get a snack when Mamma started
yelling about how she's responsible for this family and she has
to make the decisions. Gramma Patty, with a deadly seriousness,
said she has always tried to keep this a good Christian household, and after last time, Mamma promised "never again," but
now here they were. And Mamma said it worked last time, and
Gramma Patty couldn't argue with that. And Gramma Patty
said to her, "Honey, you are playing with powers beyond what
you know, and it is dangerous. It was dangerous then, and it
is now. How can you be sure that what Miss Pierre did back
then isn't the reason we're having all these problems now?" And

they went on like this, but I couldn't make much sense of it. Gramma Patty just kept going on about how faith in the Lord was the only answer, and sometimes He tests us but we have to remain firm. And if we go running to other kinds of power every time we get tested, that just shows our lack of faith and it's as good as inviting the Devil himself into the house. And Mamma became really furious when she said that and screamed that she didn't want to hear it. She said Miss Pierre was a good woman and there was no reason to believe otherwise, and she had made a decision and was sticking by it. And she didn't see Gramma Patty suggesting any better ideas.

Something like that, anyway.

Then Mamma took herself off to her bedroom and slammed the door dramatically, the way she always does when she gets herself worked up into a state.

That left me and Gramma Patty alone in the kitchen. I kind of just wanted to clear out of there and avoid being sucked into this drama, but Gramma Patty sat me down and made me some food and finally was like, "Look, you know how your mamma is. She gets an idea in her head, and there is no reasoning with her, no matter how foolish it is. I can't control her any more than you can, or anyone can. God knows, people have tried. So she's invited Miss Pierre here and I guess she's going to come and we just have to make the best of it."

Then she started going on about Miss Pierre, and honestly it didn't really clear anything up, but I guess I got the idea that, in Gramma Patty's mind anyway, Miss Pierre is some kind of witch or voodoo lady or something. And that Mamma invited her here to do magic spells on the house. I guess that explains why people in church avoid her. Pretty sure the pastor doesn't approve of that kind of stuff. Gramma Patty was trying to warn me and was telling me to be careful around her. That just having her around could encourage evil spirits to bother us. I don't know about that. I'm not even all the way certain of the stuff they talk about at church, and whether any of it is real. As for this kind of thing, I always assumed it was just superstition. I didn't even know my mamma believed in voodoo and stuff like that! Not that it's surprising. Mamma does have a tendency to get all kinds of ideas in her head. I don't know, though. I'm not sure I believe in any of it, but I have to admit I'm curious. Miss Pierre seems so nice and normal! What's she going to do? I'm half expecting her to kill a goat on our front steps now. That would definitely be exciting.

TUESDAY, MARCH 4, 6:22 A.M. (PRIVATE)

Last night there were more strange noises around the house. It started out with dogs barking, even though there aren't any dogs that live on this block. Then the barking shifted over into growling and snarling that, at a certain point, didn't even sound doglike. But I couldn't put my finger on what other animal it could be. Sometimes it sounded kind of like a person imitating a dog, and sometimes it sounded like a dog but bigger. Much bigger. And then the doors all started banging as if there were a terrible storm whipping through town, but when I stuck my head out the window, the air was perfectly still.

I tried to ignore it and go back to sleep, but the minute I closed my eyes, I was back in the middle of those visions, being tossed from one torture scenario to the next, knowing I'd committed some terrible crime but not knowing what. When I opened my eyes, instead of going away, the pain focused itself in my side again, feeling like a running cramp but so much worse. This time it was like someone was pinching and twisting at my skin with an iron clamp.

I have to admit now, I'm glad Miss Pierre is coming. There's something definitely not right in the house. And all the praying we've done doesn't seem to be helping a bit.

TUESDAY, MARCH 4, 6:12 P.M. (PRIVATE)

Miss Pierre just left. The whole thing was . . . interesting. Not really what I was expecting.

First she walked through the house a bit and sniffed around in the corners. She did that for a while, though I can't imagine how she smelled anything but the bleach. That's all I could smell. She did say she thought the bleach was probably already making a difference.

Then she talked with Mamma a bit about the energy in the house. She said the bleach was helping, but there was still something lingering. Something underneath. Mamma got a little offended at that, but Miss Pierre shushed her with a laugh. She said she wasn't talking about old food or some dead possum in the walls. It's just that houses get a particular smell when something has lodged in them. She didn't know how to describe it except as a kind of darkness. A little bitter, a little acrid. With an undertone of rot. That's how she can tell when there's an infestation. But she said not to worry, that she had smelled a lot worse. If she hadn't been paying attention, she wouldn't have even noticed it. Sometimes, she said, you walk up the front stairs to a house and you have to turn right around and walk back to the street because the stink is so powerful, it turns you away like a wall. But she was positive there was something here, and she said we were wise to take care of it early, before things turned worse.

Then she lit some herbs wrapped up in a little bundle, and in the air she drew a cross with the smoke while saying a little prayer. That helped cover the smell of the bleach a lot, actually, which was good. Next she pulled out a bottle of olive oil and poured a little onto her fingertips. Then she walked around the house, drawing crosses in olive oil on all the doors.

Before that, Gramma Patty had been looking on disapprovingly but not saying anything. Around this time, I guess she couldn't hold her tongue anymore, because she pulled Mamma into the kitchen and they started having words. I didn't want to deal with that, so I decided to follow Miss Pierre around the house to watch her work. Without really thinking about it, I started to take photos of the crosses she was drawing on the doors. When I turned around and saw Miss Pierre watching me, I suddenly got embarrassed, like she'd caught me. I wasn't sure if maybe there was something wrong or disrespectful about taking photos of her work, but she didn't seem mad. She just smiled and asked me if I'd show her my room. Luckily, it was clean and tidy, thanks to Mamma attacking everything with bleach before.

Miss Pierre sat down on the bed, patted it for me to join her, and asked me to describe in my own words some of what had been going on. So I told her about the moths in my wigs and the waking dreams where I'm being tortured and the pains I've been having and coughing stuff up and all that. She paid close attention, and when I was done, she asked if she could anoint me. I wasn't sure exactly what that meant, but I told her, "Okay." Basically she just rubbed olive oil into my hands and then painted a cross with it on my forehead.

She asked me if I had any questions, so I asked how she knew about all this stuff. She told me about how her grandmother had grown up in the islands (actually she said, "Grand-mère," because they speak French where she grew up), where this kind of practice is more out in the open. Her grand-mère was a devout Christian her whole life, but she also knew how to deal with hexes and bad spirits, and she never saw any contradiction between the two. It was a useful skill, and people would come to her for help. And she was able to help them. Miss Pierre grew up watching her do this, and she asked a lot of questions and her *grand-mère* helped train her.

Then she told me about how she first met Mamma, and how they got to know each other. It was like hearing a family secret, but from some stranger. Only I'm not sure if it's an actual secret or just something no one ever got around to telling me.

It had to do with when I was little, and I got sent away when Mamma was having problems. I knew that much. I knew she'd been under a lot of stress and had some kind of breakdown, and the cops and social services got involved, and I wound up in foster care until Mamma got settled again. That's as much of the story as I've ever known, and I'd never thought to ask anything more than that. I didn't occur to me that there was anything more. But Miss Pierre said Mamma's troubles back then were because she thought someone she worked with had put a hex on her. So many things were going wrong in her life at that moment, she felt it had to be some ill-meaning force outside of her.

Mamma got Miss Pierre's name through some friends at church. Miss Pierre saw right away there was something in her, on her, or following her around. She said Mamma was in a bad way.

I asked Miss Pierre if Mamma was right about the hex, but she just shrugged. She said it was impossible to be sure, but she didn't think it was unlikely.

Apparently Miss Pierre is the reason Mamma got me back all those years ago. That was how she got herself stable again. But I guess even then, Gramma Patty didn't approve and said if Mamma was going to move back in with her, she had to promise not to do any of that stuff again.

Miss Pierre talked about a bunch of other stuff with me too.

Once she got me started, the questions sort of flowed out of me, and Miss Pierre never acted shocked or offended, so I just kept going and she took her time and explained everything she could.

I asked why Gramma Patty doesn't like her (which maybe was super-rude, but I got the sense Miss Pierre wouldn't mind). I didn't really get Gramma Patty's problem, since it looked to me like everything Miss Pierre was doing was in the name of Jesus. Miss Pierre explained about how there's a lot of disagreement about what counts as part of Christianity. Some folks are very suspicious of anything that doesn't come straight from the mouth of their pastor, but helping people to feel better and protect their souls is no bad thing. She said the way she sees it, all that matters is what works. "I'm not one for the theology books," she said, "but the Bible tells us Jesus himself walked among people and cast demons out of them. If it was right for him to do it, why would it be wrong for me? And if people feel better after coming to me for help, why would God disapprove of that? If He loves us, doesn't He want us to feel better?" I guess I'm going to have to think about that. I'm pretty sure the pastor and Gramma Patty would say it's blasphemous to claim to do the same kind of miracles as Jesus had. But why, if the whole point is to help people? I can't imagine Jesus would be against helping people.

When Miss Pierre got up to go, I stopped her. I had one more question I'd been wanting to ask, but I didn't know how to approach it. I hemmed and hawed for a bit, but finally I just came out with it and asked why she wanted to anoint me. "Well," she said, "it can't hurt, can it?"

"But why me?" I asked. "Why me and not Mamma? Why not Gramma Patty?"

At that point, I think Miss Pierre understood what I was

getting at, but she got quiet and didn't answer me. I asked her if she thought Mamma was right this time. Has our house or our family been hexed? She just shrugged again. So I asked, "Do you think it's something else? Something to do with me specifically?" Again, she didn't answer.

I was starting to get frustrated, which made me less careful with my questions. Finally I said, "Do you know anything about demon possession? Is it real?"

Miss Pierre nodded slowly.

"Is that what's happening to me?" I asked.

Miss Pierre looked at me a long time. Then she said, "I wouldn't rule it out."

FRIDAY, MARCH 7, 4:22 P.M. (PRIVATE)

Whatever it is Miss Pierre did the other day, I think it did help. I'm not sure if it counts as magic or prayer or just psychology, but I've had a good couple of days. Just going to school and talking to friends and feeling normal. It's nice. I haven't felt this way in a while.

It's kind of like coming back to your hometown after traveling to far-off, exotic places. It's a little hard to find your footing again back in the ordinary world. Hard to remember what I used to do every day, what used to occupy my thoughts, when I wasn't worrying about hexes and demons and the state of my eternal soul.

I should start singing again. There's still time to get my voice back into shape before that audition. I'm just not feeling it though. I don't know why, but right now it seems like a lot of energy and effort I just don't have. And singing never felt that way before.

Maybe I should post something publicly on the blog. At least let people know how I am. Maybe a new tutorial. Feels sort of pointless now though. It's been so long since I made a real post, I don't think I have more than a couple of followers anymore. Everyone's moved on.

I don't blame them, to be honest. That stuff just doesn't seem as important as it once did. Lately I can't be bothered to do more than a head wrap before school. I don't get off on people looking at me the way I used to. The only thing that really holds my attention right now (outside of my own problems) is the news about the Robinson trial, and all the protests in front of the courthouse. Mamma doesn't want me to go join the protesters. She says it's too dangerous for someone my age. I don't see how it could be dangerous. They're peaceful protests! Everyone down there just wants justice and accountability. They're good people. But Mamma says with so many people gathered in one place, you don't know what could happen, especially with so many cops nearby, keeping an eye on the situation. She called it a recipe for disaster, and said everyone out there was tempting fate. Maybe so, but I think she's paranoid. Who's going to do anything to those protesters in broad daylight, around hundreds of witnesses? You'd never get away with it.

Maybe I should go down there, no matter what Mamma says. So what if it is dangerous? At least it wouldn't be boring. And I'd be doing something real. Being part of something bigger and more important than myself.

I don't know, though. Is that a real, sincere interest? Or am I just addicted to having some kind of drama in my life, and that's the most dramatic thing going on around me?

SATURDAY, MARCH 8, 10:28 A.M. (PRIVATE)

Now that the smell of bleach has faded a bit, I think I know what Miss Pierre was talking about with the smells of this house. If I think about it, I can pick up a kind of bitter scent, like something burning. A couple of times I've woken up in the middle of the night to something smelling just a little rotten. I check my pillows, my blankets, under the bed, but I can't trace it to anywhere in particular. And if I get up to get myself a glass of water, the smell seems to follow me.

But it's not just that. Sometimes I notice good smells too. I was checking over my wigs the other day, and I could swear I smelled something sweet, like flowers. Lilac, maybe, or clover? I'm not sure; I'm a city girl. Most flower smells I only know from artificial perfumes and stuff. But this wasn't like that. There was something really fresh and clean about it, and not chemical clean, like a laundry detergent. I asked Mamma if she had put in a new air freshener or gotten one of those candles, but she said no.

And then sometimes there's a smell, and I can't tell whether it's the good kind or the bad kind. It's like they're both mixed together to create something totally different, and I can't even tell whether I like it or not. It just smells complicated. And strange. I wonder what Miss Pierre would have to say about that.

MONDAY, MARCH 10, 5:48 P.M. (PRIVATE)

I guess Mamma might have been right about the protests. They were just saying on the news that there have been some outbreaks of violence in the past couple of days. The crowd got too big for the public park it was occupying, and some of the protestors moved into another area. The police told people to disperse, there was some conflict, and a bunch of people got hit with pepper spray. Things escalated from there, and some people are hurt pretty bad. Maybe it's just as well I wasn't there.

In less depressing news: I might have traced where that sweet smell was coming from. There's an old rosebush outside my bedroom window that I forgot all about because it hasn't bloomed in years. It's half dead because no one ever looks after it. It was here when Gramma Patty moved in, and none of us have much of a green thumb.

I was walking to school today though and noticed it was blooming! Loads of big heavy flowers in pink and white and yellow. I've never seen the bush bloom like that before.

WEDNESDAY, MARCH 12, 4:38 P.M. (PRIVATE)

I've been taking photos again . . . of anything that catches my attention, really. Mostly it's been stuff I see around town, or even around the house. Here's one from my last walk.

I'm not sure why I'm photographing this stuff, since no one else wants to see it, but it's something to do, at least.

Maybe I should go ahead and post them publicly. It's not like anyone could tell the difference anymore between the pictures I take and the ones that ghost or stalker or whatever used to post. I could just run with it and have my new aesthetic be "creepy dead and decaying things."

THURSDAY, MARCH 13, 4:37 P.M. (PRIVATE)

On my way home from the bus stop today, I saw a dead bird by the side of the road. I stopped to take a picture of it, like I've done before, but this time was different. I was just looking over my phone at it and I became overcome by this sense of . . . It's hard to describe. But the creature was so beautiful; the feathers were so glossy and shiny, I got swept up by an irresistible impulse to reach out and touch it. So there I am, crouching on the ground, touching this dead bird. First with my fingertips, and then I let my whole hand stroke its feathers, down its neck and along its broken wing. Writing about it here, I sound crazy. Who sits in the middle of a street, petting a dead animal? Once upon a time, I would have been disgusted by the very idea, and if I even walked near it, I'd be worried about parasites and diseases getting on me, and I'd rush home to wash my hands. But at the time, I didn't think about any of that. My mind was almost blank, and all I was really aware of was the feel of those smooth, cool feathers against my skin.

But then . . . I don't know. I really can't explain what happened next. I was so sure the bird was dead. Its neck and wing looked broken; there was blood on the pavement. A few flies buzzing around. And it felt cool under my fingers. But as I sat there, stroking it, I noticed it started to feel warmer. I thought it must be the heat from my hand warming it, but then I felt a strange thudding, and the wing was moving. Twitching.

Part of me was freaked out, and like a movie in my head, I saw myself snap my hand back and step away from the animal. But that's not what I did. I stayed there with it and felt the wing move under my hand, and I pressed down harder on it. I don't know what I was trying to do. I felt this surge of power run through me, like a tingling in my blood, and I felt like if I just kept pressing harder and harder, I could crush this fragile body into bits. So there I was, torn between two impulses: one, to jump up and get as far away from this creature as possible, and the other to press it into the pavement until I could feel the bones crunch beneath me. Instead of doing either one, I just sat there, motionless, my hand heavy on its body, my blood surging hot and feverish, and I felt that wing twitch again. And again. And then it was beating itself against the ground. I started stroking down its back again, and I could feel all the tiny muscles and bones moving together.

And then it was flying. There was a noise of feathers beating the air, and I hardly blinked before the bird was high above me, flapping and gliding like any bird in the world. I can't even begin to explain it.

What does it mean? I could have sworn that bird was dead. And now it's not. Is that because of me? Or some power using me? Would it work on other things? Like what about that rosebush? Or now that I think of it, the mold in the bathroom that just won't stay dead. Would it work on a bigger animal? What about a person?

No. No, I can't think this way. It's a coincidence; it has to be. That bird was sick; that's all. Stunned, maybe, like it ran into something and got knocked to the ground. And I just happened by at the right time. That's crazy, but any other explanation is a lot crazier. And more terrifying.

MONDAY, MARCH 17, 4:17 P.M. (PRIVATE)

I thought I was all cured from whatever was wrong with me when Miss Pierre came and did her thing, but I'm wondering now if it was only a temporary fix. I'm not sure if it's related or if it's just a bad mood or whatever, but I've been feeling all out of sorts lately. I thought it was just boredom or irritation or normal teen angst, but it's getting worse, I think. More than I can ignore.

I've been having nightmares again, about torture and pain, and I wake up, shaking and retching. There's never really any plot or story to the dreams. Just the same disturbing images they've been all along, almost like someone's flipping channels on a TV. Only, it's not like movies or TV shows, because it all feels so *real*.

It used to be that the pain would disappear as soon as I woke up, but lately the pain I feel in the dream sticks to me even after

I wake up. I'm lying there in bed, my eyes open, and my skin is so hot, it feels like it's on fire. Last night I was actually surprised when I looked down and the bed wasn't on fire. Or sometimes it's that same horrible stabbing pain in my side. I can't figure out what it is. Gramma Patty taught me to figure out the difference between muscle pain, nerve pain, bone pain, and skin pain, but this doesn't feel like any of that somehow.

I don't know how to deal with this. For as long as I can remember, music was always my refuge when anything bad was going on in my life. All I had to do was put on my headphones, and I could slip away into another world where everything was sweet and beautiful. But that doesn't work now. It's not just that I can't sing anymore; I can't listen to music either. I put my headphones on and press play, and my head is filled with screaming and wailing like I never heard before in all my life. And I swear it has to be the sounds of Hell.

Now I'm almost feeling guilty because I know I was just complaining about being bored with a normal life before all this started back up. I had been thinking I sort of liked it because it made me feel special, like I always wanted to be. But now that it's happening again . . . I don't want to be this kind of special. I'd rather just be ordinary.

I don't know what to do about this. I think I should tell someone—Mamma or Renee or Miss Pierre—but I don't know. Maybe not yet. I don't want to worry them or cause any trouble. I mean, it's not like anyone seems to know any way to cure it or make it go away. So what's the point in bringing it up over and over?

TUESDAY, MARCH 18, 3:03 P.M. (PRIVATE)

I got sent home from school today. I guess it was pretty bad. I don't exactly remember what happened, but the nurse told me when I came to that I must have had some kind of seizure. My friends say it was scary. That my body went rigid and my eyes were glassy and I didn't respond to anyone calling my name or touching me. Then I went down hard, slamming to the floor, shaking and making noises like I was choking.

I don't remember any of that at all. All I remember is that I was taking a history test when my vision went sort of wobbly. The whiteboard at the front of the class started billowing like a sail, and when I turned my head, everything else in the room looked like it was bubbling or sagging, even people's faces. And my hearing was messed up too. Everything sounded slow and underwater, except for this really intense high-pitched buzzing noise. I didn't know what to do. I just sat there, not trusting myself to move or speak. But I realized at some point that other people had noticed. I think I was gurgling or something, because everyone turned to look at me, which just made everything worse.

I couldn't stand to look at their faces. These people I've known for years suddenly looked strange and awful. I smelled smoke and fire, and that was when I really got scared. I wanted to yell and warn everyone, but I couldn't. I felt my throat close up, and I couldn't move my body, either. And it was incredibly hot. The visual distortions I was seeing were from wave after wave of heat from this terrible fire. The floor and the desks all started to melt, and the smoke was burning my eyes, and the smell of burning plastic was everywhere. And still my classmates just sat there, staring at me, sometimes moving their mouths, but I couldn't hear them. I couldn't hear the fire, either, even though I could smell it and feel it and see its effects. I didn't hear crackling or snapping like you expect from a fire. I didn't hear anything at all.

Then everything went black, and the next thing I remember, I was waking up in the nurse's office. Gramma Patty came and got me, and now I'm sitting at home. I don't know what I'm supposed to be doing, exactly. I don't feel sick, or like I need rest. If anything, I feel weirdly energized. Are they going to let me go back to school tomorrow?

TUESDAY, MARCH 18, 4:43 P.M. (PRIVATE)

I just got off the phone with Tanya, who was sitting next to me in history class. She told me what happened today at school, filling in more details. She says before I fainted, I was making all kinds of weird noises she'd never heard come out of a person before. Weird cries that were so high-pitched, they hurt her ears, or so low-pitched, she could feel the vibrations in her bones. She said I fell to my knees and started coughing and retching until I vomited onto the floor. The teacher ran over and sent someone to get help, but while they were waiting, someone noticed that the mess next to my desk didn't look normal. Even though it was kind of gross, she leaned in to look at it more closely and saw . . . Well, she said it looked like petals. Like from a whole rose, in fact, or maybe more than one—the petals were in a whole range of colors, from pinkish-yellow to a red

so deep, it was almost black. And she said at first she was holding her breath, because she expected it to smell like vomit, but
when she took a small breath by accident, she realized it smelled
sweet, not foul. "Like the inside of a flower shop," she said.

Well, if that isn't the strangest thing I ever heard. Tanya can
be kind of a drama queen and is known to exaggerate, so I wasn't
sure what to make of her story. But then she sent me a picture
from her phone.

What am I going to do? If Miss Pierre can't help me, who
can?

Renee came to see me today after school. I used to get so excited when she came to visit because we always had fun together. Now she just makes me nervous. I guess I still believe she means well, but I'm so afraid anything I say to her is going to make her take me away from Mamma.

She heard about what happened in school the other day and wanted me to talk about it. I tried to play it off as no big deal. I was in the middle of a test, I told her, and I freaked out a little. It happens. People get panic attacks. But she wasn't having it. She said people get panic attacks if they are under a ton of stress. She pointed out I don't normally panic during tests. So what new stress was I under?

I said I didn't want to talk about it, but that didn't go over well. She started prodding again about abuse, mistreatment, drugs, and then she said some of the people she talked to at my school said I was making noises—shouting and babbling, and no one could tell what I was saying. Like speaking in tongues. I didn't know what to say to that.

I had to tell her *something*, so I talked about the protests. About how I've been watching them on TV and getting a little obsessive maybe, and how Mamma and Gramma Patty are worried about it. She said she understood completely, and even admitted she's been getting a little obsessed too, and feeling both like she needs to help and like she doesn't know what she can do. At least she's an adult, and can direct her own life. She's gone over to the park a few times and brought bottled water to the protesters. I wish I could do something like that. I asked her to talk to Mamma about it, maybe get her to let me go with Renee to help out. She said she would think about it, but I'm pretty sure she means no. I think, ultimately, Renee agrees with Mamma that it's too dangerous for a kid. But you know, I'm not *really* a kid. I mean, it's not like I'm twelve! I feel like if I'm old enough to want to do it, I'm old enough to be trusted with the risks. It's not like I don't understand them.

We talked about that for a while, and I think Renee would have been satisfied with that as the only thing bothering me, except then she asked how my singing was going, and I was like, "Oh, I haven't even thought about that lately." Renee made a big deal of that, pointing out I've been obsessed with being a singer for as long as she's known me. She asked if there was something else on my mind, and I must have hesitated or made a face or something, because she jumped on it. And I just . . . I hate hiding things from her. I'm no good at it.

I really did try not to say anything too specific, but well, I don't know. I know what Mamma said about Renee's threats, but I guess I still believe she means well and wouldn't do anything to hurt me, or any of us. And she did promise she wasn't going to do anything drastic. She said the main reason she comes around is to make sure everything is okay and stable. That she's not the bad guy, not out to get anyone. What she wants personally, and what it's her job to ensure, is our family stays whole and healthy and happy.

I don't think she's lying when she says that. I want to believe her anyway. She talked about how it's her job to keep track of all the little problems before they turn into big ones. She talked about what happened with Mamma when I was a baby. How she had a lot of problems, a lot of responsibilities, and no one was helping her. She didn't know who she could turn to, so things got worse and worse until she couldn't do it anymore.

Renee said the reason she comes and talks to us is to help keep that from happening. To see the problems and help solve them before they get that bad. And so far, she's done a pretty good job. And she let me in on a secret: it might look like we'd never faced any major problems, but we had, and she and Mamma and Gramma Patty had kept them from me.

That shocked me a bit. How could there be stuff going on in my own household that I didn't know about?

Renee was quiet for a minute, letting me absorb everything, and then she said, "Laetitia, I can't help if I don't know what's wrong. I can't spot the problems if you won't talk to me and be honest."

That broke me down, and I wound up telling her stuff that has been stressing me out. Stuff Mamma told me not to talk about with her. I hope that doesn't come across as a betrayal, but I'm pretty desperate these days. I didn't know what else to do. I hoped she'd be able to help.

It's hard to come out and admit to something most people think is so crazy. That in itself wouldn't be so bad—all my life people thought I was crazy for thinking I could be a singer. But this is different. I guess it's not being called crazy I'm afraid of, but the idea that I might have something terrible in me. That I might be beyond any kind of help or salvation.

I don't think I've ever come out and said it here, in my locked entries. I might as well start now. Maybe writing it down will help me face it. Avoiding it certainly isn't helping the situation. Okay, here goes.

I'm worried I'm possessed by a demon.

Writing that sent a weird feeling through my body. A shudder. Or am I just imagining it? Am I being dramatic? Or is there something in me? Why is it so hard to tell?

Well, I told Renee. The weird thing is, she didn't act as shocked as I expected her to. She just nodded a little to herself, and her expression looked almost . . . angry. Or frustrated, maybe. Or maybe just sad. Then she asked if Miss Pierre had come around.

I didn't expect Renee to know anything about Miss Pierre, but it makes sense. Miss Pierre helped Mamma out when she had her troubles all those years ago, and that's when Renee started coming. But if Miss Pierre is the one who cured Mamma of her problem and got her back on track, why would Renee have a problem with her? They were on the same side.

But I guess it's a little more complicated than that. Renee doesn't trust Miss Pierre, and she never has. She considers her a charlatan who preys on the desperate and gullible. People who are "particularly susceptible to her brand of hokum." I didn't think that was fair, and it didn't mesh with my experiences with Miss Pierre. She helped Mamma and she was helping me. Wasn't that proof her expertise was useful? And even if it was all just fake, as long as it works and makes people feel better, where is the harm?

Renee said she's known people who have been bankrupted by Miss Pierre, or close to it. She said Mamma was lucky her "cure" came quickly, but other people go back again and again, and she never seems to fix them entirely but always offers a promise of how it will work next time. Each time, she gets to charge a new fee. I hadn't even thought about whether or not Miss Pierre was making money off this.

But how could that be her fault? She's not making these visions happen, not making the strange objects come out of my body. All that started happening before I even met her. And everything she has said and done has seemed to be with the intention of helping me. But that's true of Renee, too. So who do I believe?

I asked if I shouldn't talk to Miss Pierre anymore, but Renee said she wouldn't try to stop us from going to her. She talked about respecting people's beliefs, even when they were different from her own. But she warned me to be careful with Miss Pierre, and to contact her if anything makes me uncomfortable or suspicious. I guess that's fair enough.

Renee did say she would come by more often to make sure nothing gets too out of hand. Maybe Renee will see that Miss Pierre's work helps us, and it will change her mind.

SATURDAY, MARCH 22, 2:33 P.M. (PRIVATE)

Mamma and Gramma Patty are driving me crazy! They're treating me like a little kid, making me leave my laptop and my phone in the living room so they can keep an eye on me when I go online. They haven't been this strict in years! But I guess they figured out I was sneaking on to find information about the Robinson trial.

I know they're just worried about me, but I wish they could see it's the only thing that distracts me from my own problems and makes me think about bigger things than myself. It just kills me that it's all going on practically on my doorstep, but I'm being kept in the dark about it.

Mamma and Gramma Patty have gotten way more intense about their rules and restrictions over the past couple of days. Makes me wonder if there's something specific they don't want me to know. But what could it be?

SUNDAY, MARCH 23, 11:39 A.M. (PRIVATE)

Something is really wrong. I don't even know where to begin.

Gramma Patty made me go to church again, and at first it was okay. I was a little annoyed to be there, but there was nothing out of the ordinary. Then the pastor started talking about the Robinson trial and the protestors, and I know now why Mamma and Gramma Patty were trying to keep me away from the news. At first he was just going through the usual thing he does every week, mentioning people from the congregation who are sick or lost their jobs or whatever, and asking everyone to pray for them. I was barely paying attention. Then he was talking about the Robinson protestors, and he mentioned that a big group of them had been arrested earlier this week, and some hadn't been able to make bail yet. He was asking people to pray for a speedy release. He read off a pretty long list of names, and guess who was on it. . . . Malcolm.

I was pretty upset when I heard. Worried about Malcolm of course, and also feeling guilty that my name *wasn't* on that list. I instantly felt like I should have been there with them. It sickens me to think of myself sitting at home, eyes glazing over, reading all this stupid commentary, when people like Malcolm are actually out there, making a difference.

Then the choir started up, and at first it was fine. Then I realized they were all singing, but I couldn't really hear their voices. It was like they were singing underwater or something. I started to worry I was having another panic attack or episode or whatever, and worrying only ever makes it worse. So I started panicking, my heart was racing, my palms sweating, my vision going black at the edges, and I blinked a few times to clear it, and all of a sudden the scene changed in front of me. The singing came back like someone flicked a volume switch, only it wasn't singing that was coming out of their mouths—it was shrieking and moaning and crying, like all of them were in the worst kind of pain. And they weren't swaying energetically to whatever hymn; they were being dragged this way and that by beasts. Little monsters with animal faces and pointed ears and blue-tinted flesh. Some of the little demons were grabbing their arms or holding their robes, some were beating them with short sticks, and others were blowing thick heavy smoke into their eyes.

That was when I realized the choir members weren't just screaming; they were calling to me to help them and save them from this torture. Part of me knew this probably wasn't real, but I couldn't just sit there and watch it, so I jumped up and ran from the church and out into the hallway. A terrible wave of nausea took me, and I feel to my knees, the muscles of my esophagus convulsing. It was so painful. Much more painful than vomiting normally is. I managed to cough something up and spit it out onto the floor. I retched a few more times until the feeling passed, and then I opened my eyes. The little pile in front of me was smooth and sharp and covered in blood and bile, so I wasn't sure what it was. And as I stared at it, another spasm moved through my body, and I felt another object coming up, and another, and I realized what I was looking at were shards of broken glass. I have no idea how my body could possibly have produced something like that. And every time I thought it was done, it just kept coming and coming.

Eventually I realized there was a crowd standing around me, and Mamma had her arm around my back, and Gramma Patty was trying to shoo them all away. At one point I looked up and saw Miss Pierre, who looked very worried.

I don't know what all this is, but it can't be good.

SUNDAY, MARCH 23, 8:19 P.M. (PRIVATE)

After Miss Pierre saw what happened at church, she called
Mamma to set up another appointment. I was in bed but could
hear Mamma on the phone and, from her answers, I could tell
who she was talking to. I was surprised when she turned down
Miss Pierre's offer and said the social worker might cause trouble
if she found out.

I know I was saying before I wasn't sure if Miss Pierre's
methods were working, but no one is offering me anything better right now! So I asked Mamma to let Miss Pierre come. I'll
deal with Renee if she has a problem with it, but we've got to
do something. I can't keep living like this.

Miss Pierre visited today after school. She says she underestimated the problem last time, but she seemed to think she had a few more tricks up her sleeve. Last time she believed the problem was in the house, but after the incident at the church, she was convinced that whatever entity is bothering us is centered on my body. And that requires a different approach.

I couldn't help thinking about what Renee had said about Miss Pierre deliberately leading us on and dragging this out, so I got Miss Pierre alone and asked about it. It was awkward, but I needed to know. I think I offended her a bit when I asked if it was right for her to charge people for what she does. "Why shouldn't I charge?" she said. "You don't expect a plumber to come fix your pipes for free. Or an exterminator to get rid of your termites for free. I have to make a living like anyone else.

My skill and learning are valuable to people, so why shouldn't I support myself with it?"

I guess that does make sense. I couldn't think of any response to it. Anyway, Mamma told me later that Miss Pierre didn't accept payment this time, since she felt she should have done more before. She only asked for reimbursement for supplies. I wonder if she did that because of what I'd said. I'd feel bad if she suffered because of my suspicions.

The supplies she mentioned were for a little altar she set up in my room. That's the only way to describe it. It's an overturned milk crate with a white towel over it, some candles with pictures of saints on them, a crucifix, and a bible open to Psalm 91. She spread salt all around the edge of the room, which seems kind of dirty to me, but she said it would help keep evil spirits away. The problem with that is, it sorta seems like there's already an evil spirit following me around, or maybe even inside of me. So how can the salt protect me if there's a demon already in me? Unless maybe the salt isn't meant to protect me. Maybe it's meant to protect everyone else *from* me.

Even though it feels a little weird, I do feel better with the altar set up. With the candles going, it's almost like having a night-light. And it's hard to imagine demons tormenting me with a bible right nearby.

Gramma Patty is not a big fan of Miss Pierre's altar. I didn't really get why. It's got a bible and everything. How can she claim it's unchristian? But she doesn't like the candles with pictures of saints on them. She called the altar black magic. I don't see how it can be black magic if loads of pretty normal people have saints as part of their religion. It's not like Devil worship or something. But it might as well be if you ask Gramma Patty. She says our church doesn't worship anyone but God, and the pastor would have a fit if he knew.

She wanted the whole altar out of the house right away, but Mamma convinced her to let me keep it for a while. Who knew this stuff was so complicated? The way I've always seen it is, *Love God; avoid the Devil.* Should be simple enough. But when people can't even agree on what's on God's side and what's on the Devil's, how am I supposed to sort it out? All I know is that Miss Pierre's altar makes me feel safer.

But then again, if I *am* possessed by some demon, maybe my instincts aren't to be trusted. . . .

WEDNESDAY, MARCH 26, 6:46 P.M. (PRIVATE)

Renee visited again today and made a bit of a fuss about the altar. I thought she said she was okay with Miss Pierre's techniques. . . . Whatever happened to live and let live? I don't know. She seemed pretty upset about it. She made me tell her everything Miss Pierre had said, down to the last word. I felt like I was being interrogated by the police. I guess she just wanted to see how much Mamma and I were being brainwashed by Miss Pierre. I really don't think we are, though! We're just in a bad situation, and getting help the only place we know.

I guess I managed to convince her, because she let it drop. She just made me promise not to leave the candles lit when I went to sleep. She said they're a fire hazard and are too dangerous. I agreed, but I think she's being paranoid. The candles are wrapped in glass, and they aren't easy to knock over. Loads of people leave them burning all night. That's whole point. But it seemed easier to just agree with her in the moment. I guess it's a fair compromise.

She also asked me if I'd be willing to see a psychiatrist. She seemed like she expected me to be really put off by the idea, but I don't know. . . . Anything that's helpful at this point can only be good. And maybe I *am* crazy. People always act like that would be the worst thing in the world, but look at my alternatives. If it turns out I'm crazy, that I've been secretly faking this whole thing, it would be a relief, in a way. Something that could be treated with pills, and I'd be back to my old self. I'd pick that over having my soul claimed by a demon, that's for sure. So I said okay.

FRIDAY, MARCH 28, 3:40 P.M. (PRIVATE)

Back from my appointment with the psychiatrist. It was all right, I guess. Not as satisfying as I expected. I didn't realize I'd been expecting anything at all, but everything I know about psychiatrists comes from movies and stuff, so I guess I'd been picturing something like that. I thought it would be a lot of talking about my feelings, and that I would get a chance to go into a lot of detail about my situation, and she'd make me play word-association games and judge my responses to inkblots and stuff. In a way I was kind of looking forward to it.

But she didn't really bother with any of that. She asked me a million yes-or-no questions (and got annoyed if I gave an answer other than yes or no), most of which had nothing at all to do with my specific situation, like with the puking up glass and bones and all that. She asked about my stress levels and how I was doing in school and my sleep schedule. Stuff about eating disorders, and if I have any phobias. I wasn't sure how to answer that one. She asked if I was afraid of supernatural creatures, and I was like, "Yeah, I am," but she never asked if my fear might be based on actual experiences with supernatural creatures.

I guess that sort of thing doesn't even occur to normal people, but it all felt a little pointless, like her questions weren't getting anywhere close to the real problems in my life. But eventually the psychiatrist got around to asking me if I ever saw or heard things other people didn't, so I said yes, and she followed up a bit on that, asking me to describe them. So I told her about some of those strange visions I've had where I'm being tortured, and the stuff that happened at church and at school, and she scribbled a lot on her note pad. Then at the end she talked to Mamma for a while without me, and Mamma came out with some kind of prescription. So now I have these pills I'm supposed to take every night, but I don't even know exactly what I'm being treated for.

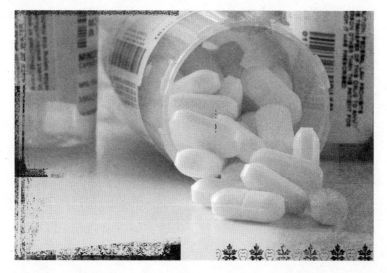

PSYCHIATRIC DIAGNOSTIC REPORT

Performed by: ~~███████~~

Patient: L————

Date of Examination: 3/28/2014

Patient presents as psychologically unstable. Reports severe visual, auditory, and tactile disturbances and hallucinations, coupled with persistent delusions of persecution and grandiosity, suggestive of possible early onset schizoaffective disorder. Otherwise, largely asymptomatic. Recommend course of antipsychotic medication to be taken daily.

WEDNESDAY, APRIL 2, 10:10 P.M. (PRIVATE)

I've been taking the pills the doctor gave me, and I think I can maybe start to say they are working. I *have* felt more like myself again lately. There are some annoying side effects, but I haven't had any of those visions or torture dreams lately, or any unexplained pains. No vomiting incidents.

And I think maybe even my voice might be coming back! I was doing the dishes after dinner the other night, and Gramma Patty came in and was like, "It's so nice to hear you sing again." I hadn't even realized I was doing it! It definitely wasn't my stage voice, but for so long now I haven't been able to so much as hum. I thought that part of me was gone for good.

I don't want to push things, but maybe I'll go to the auditorium and just see what happens.

SATURDAY, APRIL 5, 8:46 A.M. (PRIVATE)

Not much to report; just wanted to note that I woke up this morning feeling pretty good! I was in a really good mood, singing in the shower, and I couldn't figure out any particular reason. Then I realized it's because I didn't have any nightmares last night! And it's been a while since I felt that pain in my side too. It's kind of sad that simply waking up after a night without pain or terror is enough to put me in a good mood.

I don't know whether it's Miss Pierre or the pills, but something seems to be working. As for singing, my voice is still a little rusty from disuse, but I'm working on it. It's hard, but it feels good.

THURSDAY, APRIL 10, 4:22 P.M. (PRIVATE)

I haven't checked in on here in a while. I guess there's not much to report these days. Everything's pretty much fine. I did pass this weird tree on the way home and decide to photograph it. I don't know why, I was just drawn to it. I guess it's all just part of my "dead and dying things" aesthetic.

SUNDAY, APRIL 13, 2:12 P.M. (PRIVATE)

Something weird happened at church today. I was killing time after the service while Mamma and Gramma were making the rounds, saying hello to everyone. I ducked into one of the back rooms where I used to get ready before choir practice. Mrs. Matthews, who sometimes helps clean up the church, was back there. She told me she'd seen a rat last Sunday, so she'd put out some poison and was checking to see if it got anything.

She gave me the strangest look when I asked if I could help her check. I guess normal teenage girls aren't so quick to help clean up dead rats. I don't know why I offered. The words were out of my mouth before I even thought about them. I just don't see the point in hiding from the uglier side of the world, and pretending death and vermin and suffering don't exist. I'd rather look them in the face.

Mrs. Matthews just shrugged and said, "Suit yourself," so I followed her down and checked the corners as she shined a flashlight around. We found one rat lying stiff and cold under the stairs, so I took an old towel from Mrs. Matthews and used it to pick him up. She was standing there, holding a big sack open, and all I had to do was unwrap the towel and drop him in, but for a few seconds I couldn't do it. I was clutching the towel in my hand, and it was like my fingers just wouldn't open. Mrs. Matthews got annoyed and asked what I was waiting for, and that was when I realized the towel was warm.

I didn't know what to do. I held it clutched in my hands for a few seconds, too stunned to let it go. The next thing I knew, the critter was twitching in my fingers, and Mrs. Matthews let out a scream to wake the dead. That shocked me out of my daze, my hands opened, the bundle fell to the floor, and what do you know? The little beast wriggled for a second and then scampered away.

I looked up, and Mrs. Matthews was staring at me like she'd just seen the Devil himself. "That rat was dead," she said. "Poisoned. What did you do?" I didn't have any answer. She shook her head and backed away from me, muttering about how something wasn't right about me. That I'd better get away from her.

The worst thing is, I know she's right. I may not understand it, but even I can see there's something very wrong with me.

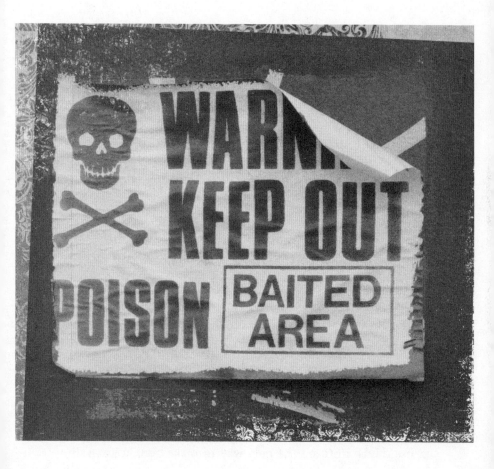

MONDAY, APRIL 14, 4:02 P.M. (PRIVATE)

It just came on the news—they're going to announce the verdict of the Robinson trial today! I can't remember when I've ever been so nervous about anything. And I just rewatched the video. There's no way they could find those policemen anything but guilty, right? Gramma Patty is worried about what will happen if it goes the other way. Worried there will be riots. I can't help thinking, if the system is that broken, maybe there *should* be riots. Maybe riots are the only way to make people listen. But Gramma Patty and Mamma both give me worried looks if I talk like that, so I try to keep my opinions to myself. In any case, I think Gramma Patty is worried for nothing because I really don't see how any sensible person could watch that video and think the policemen are innocent. I'm sure the jury made the right decision.

MONDAY, APRIL 14, 5:10 P.M. (PRIVATE)

Not guilty. I don't believe it. I just don't believe it.

MONDAY, APRIL 14, 7:26 P.M. (PRIVATE)

I still just can't even believe it about the trial. I have so many feelings about this that I don't know how to sort them out. I'm just so disappointed. And outraged. And shocked. And just . . . sad. It still seems impossible to believe. I still feel like I'm going to wake up tomorrow morning and find out they haven't given the verdict yet, and it was all a bad dream. How can this be reality? Even with all the crazy stuff I've been dealing with, at least that's just me and my family. I always took comfort in the fact that the real world still made sense, and everything works more or less the way I expect and understand.

But now this, which just seems as crazy as anything that has happened. There was a video! How could the jury watch it and not see what happened? How could they not see it as clearly as I did?

I'm so twisted up and upset over this. Just sad and angry and guilty, I guess. Which is weird, I know. Why should I feel guilty? I wasn't on the jury; I didn't shoot Dwayne Robinson. What does any of it have to do with me? How could I possibly have influenced the decision of a bunch of jury members I've never even met? But I feel like I should have done more. I should have gone to those demonstrations. I should have prayed.

But I couldn't. I guess that's what's freaking me out.

Just before they made the announcement, Mamma suggested we all join hands and pray about it. Gramma Patty asked me to lead the prayer, and I couldn't. I started to, but I only got about halfway through before my throat closed up and no sound came out. It was just like with the singing, when this all started. Only it was more than that. It wasn't just that my voice died; my mind went blank too. My brain just emptied, and I couldn't go on.

I just looked up and stared at Gramma Patty and Mamma like an idiot. Gramma Patty saw and squeezed my hand a little, and then she took over and finished the prayer and it was fine. I felt relieved, like she'd saved it, and nothing really bad had happened. I just chalked it up to nerves about the trial, and being overexcited.

But then the announcement came, and how could I avoid thinking about what had happened? How could I help making a connection? That my failure to speak that prayer was a failure of faith somehow, and that failing is the reason why God turned his back on the Robinson family and refused to give them justice.

I know; that's ridiculous. It doesn't work like that. Why would God do something so cruel and pointless? But that doesn't make this bad feeling go away.

I can't stop watching the news. Even Mamma and Gramma Patty are too obsessed now to remember to stop me. It's still surreal to watch them describe what's going on even as I can hear it happening only a few blocks away.

A huge crowd has gathered outside the courthouse, more than twice the usual number of protesters. For now everything's still pretty peaceful, but no one knows when the tension might break. It feels like we're right on the edge of something major. Everyone knows something's gonna happen, but no one knows exactly what or when, how long it will last, what might touch it off, or what the damage will be. Gramma Patty can't stop moaning about how it's always our own community that suffers from these things. Buildings will burn, shopkeepers forced out of business by looters, people made homeless by the destruction.

She has lived through stuff like this before, and even Mamma has seen it on TV, but this is all new to me. I don't know what to expect.

All I can think is that I should be down there. I should be there at the courthouse, protesting this sad mockery of justice and making my voice heard. But there's no way Mamma and Gramma Patty would allow that. They say it's too dangerous, and there's no telling what harm I might come to. But someone has to speak out!

For now all I can do is hole up here, reloading the news on my laptop and listening for sirens.

TUESDAY, APRIL 15, 3:13 A.M. (PRIVATE)

Just woke up from an awful nightmare. . . .

At first it was the same as usual, with the wheel and the grill and the arrows and the iron spike. Those are becoming like old friends now. Then the scene shifted. There were horses trapped in a burning barn, and I was trying to get the door open to let them out, but I couldn't figure out the latch. Then it switched over to something else. I felt better because it was outside at least. I was caught up in a herd of animals who were stampeding across a field or prairie, but then I saw a machine looming ahead of us, gleaming in the moonlight, and I realized the animals were running toward some kind of slaughtering mechanism.

I awoke to the sound of piercing screams mixed with growl- ing and barking, and I'm still not sure if the sounds were from the dream or real life or a mixture of the two. My eyes were burning from smoke, and it sounded like a dozen different sirens were going outside. I can still hear them. If I listen hard, I can hear shouting and yelling, too. It's carrying here on the wind, even though the worst of the riots are a few miles away.

WEDNESDAY, APRIL 16, 6:53 A.M. (PRIVATE)

The city is a little calmer this morning, but I found something strange in the street in front of our house. It looks like bones from a slaughterhouse. How did they get here? Does it have something to do with all the activity last night?

THURSDAY, APRIL 17, 5:24 P.M. (PRIVATE)

Every day the riots get a little closer to our neighborhood. Mostly people have been sticking to the main roads where there are shops and things, but sometimes I run across strange overflow, even on our little street. If I take a roundabout route home from the bus stop, I pass by a lot of the wreckage.

Mamma doesn't know I do. She told me in no uncertain terms that I was to walk straight home after school every day. She and Gramma Patty even discussed walking to the bus stop to meet me so I wouldn't have to walk alone, but I told them to back off. I'm not five years old.

She doesn't know I've gone out a few times, taking photos of the way our neighborhood has been changed by the riots. I don't know why I do it, exactly. I want to do something, to make all the suffering and anger and frustration stop, but I don't know how and the adults won't let me do anything. I hate feeling so helpless and powerless.

Taking pictures is all I can think of to do, but it frustrates me because it isn't helping anyone. And I worry it's just satisfying some sick fascination with other people's misery. Like I'm feeding off them. Gramma Patty says it isn't healthy, and I think she might be right.

SATURDAY, APRIL 19, 3:22 A.M. (PRIVATE)

I really think I'm losing my mind. For a while now I've been having those nightmares, and they always felt really vivid and real, and sometimes they seemed to come on me even when I was awake, but there would always be a moment when I woke up or blinked or snapped out of it, and I'd know it was just one of those attacks.

But now there's been a shift. I started forcing myself to stay awake because I was afraid of dealing with the pain and scary images. Drinking colas and stuff, going online, watching movies, anything. But I think that might have backfired, because now the torture scenes are slipping into my everyday life, and I'm not even sure where they end and reality begins.

Mamma says she has caught me sleeping with my eyes open, and at school people have seen me walk from class to class with my eyes closed. And I see terrible things. Someone in the school yard being pelted with rocks. Someone walking down the hall, blood dripping from their forehead. A girl crushed under the wheel of a giant construction truck. What do I do? Keep walking and tell myself it's just my imagination? Or run over and try to help, only to find the bodies disintegrating through my fingers?

If I can't tell dreams from hallucinations from reality, what does it all even mean?

SATURDAY, APRIL 19, 8:42 P.M. (PRIVATE)

I thought it was bad before, but now I feel like I am losing my grip on reality. I don't know who or what I am anymore.

Tonight after dinner I was having a totally normal conversation with Mamma and Gramma Patty about an English paper I have to write, and then I just froze. In the middle of a sentence. I don't really remember what happened after that. One moment I was sitting at the kitchen table, and the next I was on the floor, that thick feeling in my throat—the one I'm now starting to recognize means I'm going to cough up something nasty. I thought I'd blacked out for just a few seconds, but later Mamma told me it was almost an hour that I was out!

Mamma says I started shaking and making strange noises, my eyes rolling back in my head. Mamma and Gramma Patty were trying to help, rubbing my back, talking to me, saying my name.

Then Mamma started praying over me, and I couldn't take it. I've heard Mamma pray probably every day of my life, but suddenly it was like every terrible sound all mixed together: nails on a blackboard and microphone feedback and a knife scratching a plate. . . . All I know is that I wanted it to *stop*, and I threw my arms out in front of me to try to push it away.

I wound up giving Mamma a mighty shove that sent both her and Gramma Patty reeling back against the wall. Mamma was shocked silent for a bit, but soon enough she started praying again, and Gramma Patty joined her. That just got me more upset, so they stopped. Mamma says that was when I started speaking in a strange voice—sometimes very quickly or slowly, sometimes in what sounded like another language. What they could understand sounded like I was describing what it was like to be tortured and killed—my eyes getting ripped out, arrows sinking into my flesh, getting run through with spikes and beaten with whips and then tied to a stake and burned alive. I had never actually told Mamma and Gramma Patty the details of my dreams, so they were all new to them.

As Mamma was telling me all this, I kept seeing these images flash before my eyes. The ones that kept appearing on my blog after every attack. The wheel. The grill. The girl with blood coming out of her eye. I don't think those images are random. I think they add up to something. That they *mean* something. But what is it all trying to tell me? Is that what this demon wants from me? To drag me to hell and torture me in all these different ways?

Mamma said I was pacing the kitchen, back and forth between them, sometimes approaching for long enough to touch their faces or stare into their eyes.

When I seemed calmer, they joined hands and tried praying again. That was when I fell to the floor, thrashing and writhing around. Mamma saw stuff moving under my skin, like some creature was pushing on me from the inside, trying to tear its way out. Then I came to. This part I remember, because I was on the floor, coughing again, and what came up were three balled-up wads of paper. They were pretty gross, but I spread them out, and sure enough, there's something written on them that looks like a weird language! Some devil language, says Mamma.

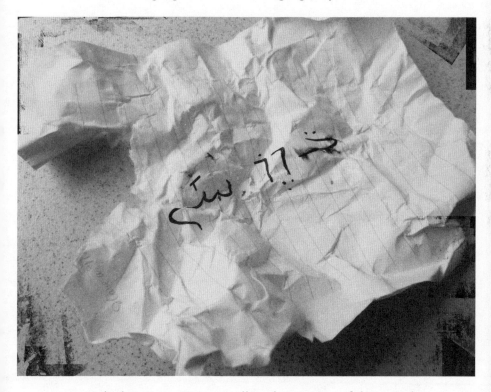

I asked Gramma Patty to tell me her version of the story, but she wouldn't talk about it. She can only say that she's worried, that it's all happening again, that "they" are going to come in here and tear this family apart. She shook her head and said, "You've got to stop this devilry, or they will take you away. You've got to fight this off and pray to the Lord, and that's the only thing that will help."

I'm starting to get really scared. Before, everything was happening *to* me. But now it's me doing the stuff, only I can't control it! What if I do something terrible while in some kind of a trance? What if I hurt someone?

Renee came by today and found me still in freak-out mode over what had happened. I didn't want to talk to her about it, but I basically had no choice. She could tell just by looking at me that something had given me a bad scare. So I told her I went into another trance, like at school and at church. Of course she wouldn't leave that alone. She wanted to know all the details. I told her I didn't remember any of it, but she kept pushing.

I really didn't want to talk about it, but Renee's not the type to take no for an answer. We talked about other things, school and the riots and stuff, but she always kept circling back, like she was trying to catch me off guard. I got frustrated and practically yelled at her, "I don't know! I don't remember!"

I told her to ask Mamma, since she was there, but she said

she wanted to hear it from me. I just told her it was like someone had taken over my body and used it for their own purposes.

Then she asked if I was still taking my medication, and I told her, "Yes, of course I am. I've missed a dose here and there, but mostly yes." She didn't like that at all. She asked exactly how many I missed, and I said I didn't remember. More than one. She told me to get the bottle and count out how many doses are left. We kind of got into a big fight then. I never used to fight with Renee, but lately I feel like she doesn't trust me. Like she's trying to control every little thing or trying to make me say things I don't want to say.

I brought all that up, but she was on a mission and wouldn't talk about anything else until I brought her the pill bottle. She counted out the pills and said I'd only taken eight when I should have taken twenty-four.

I was like, "Yeah, I forget sometimes." Then she made me go through this whole thing of trying to remember when exactly I forget to take them: what time of day, what am I doing. That kind of misses the whole point of forgetting! She had me set an alarm on my phone to remind me, and we moved the pill bottle to my bedside table instead of the bathroom, so I won't have to get up and leave the room to take them. I guess that will help.

Before she left, she talked to Mamma about how I'd been skipping my pills and how she needs to make sure I take them every night. Mamma wasn't impressed. She kept saying anyone could see there was a demon in me, and that pills weren't going to help anything. Renee got very quiet at that, and her expression was as serious as I had ever seen it. I couldn't really hear what she was saying, but I got the picture. No more talk of demons and no more visits from Miss Pierre, or else there will be big trouble.

CASE REPORT

Family

Date of Report: 4/21/2014   Date of Visit: 4/20/2014

Complainant: ███████ (Family doctor)

Family Surname: ███████

Name of child: L——

Age: 15

DESCRIPTION OF CASEWORKER VISIT:

On Sunday, April 20, I made a scheduled visit to the ██ family to check on the progress of their situation since L—— began receiving treatment for possible schizoaffective disorder three weeks ago. Unfortunately, after initial signs of improvement, L——'s symptoms seem to have worsened significantly. She is currently exhibiting severe behavioral disturbances, including disruptive and even aggressive behavior at school, as well as at home. Previously L—— has rarely been disruptive, and has no history of aggressive behavior.

It is difficult to account for what has brought about this change. L—— herself points to possible depression over her difficulty with singing and preparing for her upcoming audition, though in behavior she does not appear overly concerned with this problem anymore. She also mentions anxiety over, and preoccupation with, the recent upheaval in her neighborhood. It's possible that outbreaks of violence and destruction have caused L——'s regression to previously abandoned behavior patterns.

It is also worth noting that the only recipient of her aggression so far has been L——'s mother. This could indicate that there is some latent hostility between the two of them, even though when asked, they both profess to be intensely devoted to each other.

When asked directly about her actions, L— claims she doesn't remember them, and maintains she was in a "trance" or "blackout state" the entire time. However, upon further prodding, L— produced details and descriptions of the events that could only be known to her or suggest a certain self-awareness during the incidents (e.g. "my heart was pounding," "I was afraid I would hurt her," etc.).

L— has also been inconsistently compliant with her medication, which is presumably contributing to these episodes. We discussed strategies for making sure her medication is taken according to an appropriate schedule.

One final note: L— has repeatedly tried to direct my attention to some scraps of paper with scribbles on them, which she maintains have some significant relationship to her situation.

(These items were supposedly disgorged by her during one of her "trances.") So far I have chosen not to encourage L—'s sense that there is anything meaningful and important in these "messages." I would prefer her to abandon her reliance on these tricks and/or delusions, and confront her situation more directly. I am striving to keep our conversations focused on L—'s behavior, and not play into her preferred narrative of "demonic possession."

I remain alert to the possibility that L— is deriving some psychological or emotional benefit from these "attacks," maybe in terms of getting attention or forming a useful alliance with her mother, etc. I am working to discourage these tools, and emphasizing positive reinforcement of more productive modes of communication and family interaction.

—R. S.

TUESDAY, APRIL 22, 9:35 P.M. (PRIVATE)

The alarm on my phone just went off. The one Renee set. That means I'm supposed to take my pill. I'm sitting in bed right now, and the pills are on a little table right next to me. There's even some bottled water with them. I don't have to get up or anything. It would be the easiest thing in the world to take one. So why haven't I taken it?

Why don't I do it? Why don't I just stop typing for a few seconds, reach out, pick up the bottle, and tap one out into my hand? It would be so easy, but I'm just sitting here, typing, not doing it. I don't know. I can't explain it. I just don't want to. Is that it? Or is that I can't? Maybe there's some force stopping me. Things were getting better with the pills. Everything was headed back to normal. I was going to just be an ordinary kid again. And if I don't take them, if I skip even a few, all that scary stuff will start to come back again. Nightmares, visions, trances—who knows what else? Who knows how much worse it could get? I don't want to find out; that's for sure.

So what stops me from taking the pills when I know they will help? I told Renee I kept forgetting, but that's not really it. There were times when I'd be watching TV or playing on my phone, and I knew it was time to take my pills and I just didn't. Or even sometimes I'd be brushing my teeth, standing at the sink, the pill bottle right in front of me, and I'd just ignore it. Pretend like I didn't even see it.

Is this what it felt like for Mamma all those years ago, when the demon was harassing her? The scariest part is not knowing what's my own mind and what is some intruder. It feels like I am making my own decisions, but my decisions don't make any sense, even to myself.

Everyone wants me to take the pills. Everyone says I should do it. But they can't make me.

Ugh, this is silly! That's so immature. I can do this. I'm going to put down my laptop right now, take a pill, and go to sleep. Right now.

Soon.

WEDNESDAY, APRIL 23, 6:15 A.M. (PRIVATE)

I was in my room last night, trying not to fall asleep, when I had another one of my attacks. I haven't had one like this in a while now. I kind of hoped I was through with them, but I guess not. One minute I was sitting up in bed, watching something on my laptop, all the lights on. Then in the next . . . my eyes must have slipped closed, because everything went dark and I felt myself dragged down onto the bed by some invisible force. I tried to struggle, but something held me down so I couldn't move or make any noise. It was terrifying, but so far it wasn't painful. I hoped there wouldn't be any pain, but I knew that was wishful thinking. If there's one thing I know about these attacks, it's that they are always excruciating.

I just lay there, waiting for the pain to come in whatever form it would take. What else could I do? Just like before, there was something else before the pain: that feeling I was being punished for something. That I have done some terrible crime that has made everyone hate me, and now they're going to torture me because of it. And the worst thing is, I have no idea what I've done.

There was something different about it this time, though. I still didn't know what it was I was being punished for, but for the first time I didn't have any weight of guilt or fear associated with it. Whatever it was, I wasn't sorry at all. I was proud of it. And I knew it would bring punishment, torture, and pain—I had always known that—but I didn't care. In that strange moment, I welcomed it. It was like I *wanted* the pain, just to prove to myself I was just as terrible as everyone thought I was.

And then it came. Not in my skin this time, or my bones or my eyes. It was in my mouth. I saw in front of me a long twisted instrument like iron pliers, and the next thing I knew, some force was dragging my mouth open and applying the tool to my teeth. One by one, I felt them twist free, cracking the bones and snapping the nerves, filling my mouth and throat with thick hot blood.

The pain was the most intense I've felt so far. It wasn't just in my teeth; it was running through my whole body, like a white-hot electric current, and I trembled with it. But even as I was conscious of this agony, there was something satisfying about it. I knew I had earned this torture, and I wanted it to purify me. Over and over, the thoughts that pulsed through my mind were *yes* and *more*. I wanted to be taken apart completely.

And then, just as suddenly as it had come over me, it started to slip away. I could feel my body start to relax, and I was able to form some coherent thoughts around the slackening pain.

The sensation of blood flooding my mouth evaporated, and I ran my tongue over my teeth, half expecting to find smooth empty gums. But as far as I could tell, everything was in place.

Just as I was about convinced everything had slipped back to normal, I felt something near the back of my jaw. I prodded at it with my tongue and then stuck a finger into my mouth to clear it out. It was a tooth. A huge one. Definitely a molar, maybe a wisdom tooth. I ran to the mirror and checked and checked, but I couldn't see anything wrong with my teeth! A tooth like this . . . There's no way you could lose it without seeing the difference.

So I guess the question is: Whose tooth is it?

WEDNESDAY, APRIL 23, 6:34 A.M. (PRIVATE)

After I posted that last entry, I reloaded my blog, expecting to see a strange photo waiting for me there, like there had been all the previous times, but there was nothing there. Like my ghost had forgotten about me.

But I have a picture to post anyway. After the tooth came out, I snapped a photo of it. Maybe that's why the blog didn't produce one on its own. It's not just giving me pictures anymore; it's giving me the real thing. And I don't need some ghost showing me my worst fears when I'm the one taking the pictures now.

FRIDAY, APRIL 25, 6:14 P.M. (PRIVATE)

The riots are getting closer and more out of control. Nights are filled with the sounds of sirens mixed with the cries of the mob, and every morning there is a new path of destruction cut through the city. Mamma and Gramma Patty are terrified, but in a weird way I feel drawn to it. I wake sometimes in the night and I can feel all the energy of the mob coursing through me— their panic and their rage, but also a raw, surging sense of power. It's scary, but not exactly in a bad way. It makes my whole body tingle with excitement.

There's pain, too. I'm still getting those pains in my side. This is going to sound really nuts, but it's a good pain. Not exactly the good pain that comes from stretching before exercise, or getting a massage. It still feels fiery and hot, but I've figured out that if I don't resist it, if I don't try to push back against it, it doesn't bother me so much. And sometimes, once it starts to fade, I almost kind of miss it, and if I focus my mind, I can make it come back. So I can feel it a little longer.

Sometimes when I do that, when I close my eyes and focus on the pain, I get visions of those torture scenes again. Those, too, though—they don't scare me the way they used to. I'm fascinated by them, and sometimes they seem weirdly comforting.

See, I said it was crazy! How could pain and torture be comforting? But I don't know how else to describe it. I just feel drawn to both somehow.

I don't know what any of it means. Am I self-destructive? Or is it some demon messing with my mind, trying to tempt me into Hell?

I'm home from school again today. I wasn't feeling well this morning. It was that old skin-crawly feeling, seeing stuff in the corner of my eye, jumping at shadows. I asked Mamma if I could skip school, but she said no, I'd missed too much school already this year.

That's one of the things I could get taken away for—if the school says I haven't been showing up enough. But it's not like I'm just cutting class to go out and have fun! I've just got bigger things to deal with right now than pop quizzes. I don't have the mental energy for school.

But Mamma said she wasn't having anyone call her a bad mother for keeping her kid out of school, so I was just going to have to pull myself together. Easy for her to say!

I kind of had a little tantrum about it, which I don't normally do. Usually, if Mamma tells me to do something, I do it, and I don't answer back. But today I just *really* couldn't deal with school, so I was whining and complaining and trying to get Mamma to change her mind. Finally Gramma Patty asked if it would help if we did a prayer circle before I left. When I was a kid, that used to settle me down if I was cranky or being difficult, though it's been a while since I had much interest in that sort of thing. But I thought, well, why not? It used to make me feel better; maybe it would still work. So I said fine, and Gramma Patty and Mamma stood on either side of me and held hands around me.

As soon as they started speaking, I got this terrible throbbing pain in my head, like my skull was being forced open from the inside. For a minute I was actually scared my whole head might burst into pieces. I was groaning and crying and grabbing my head, and I remember falling to the floor, my whole body shaking and thrashing. Then Mamma and Gramma Patty stopped the prayer, and I immediately felt calmer. And I had this trickling sensation on my face, and Mamma told me my nose was bleeding.

Gramma Patty said, "Don't just stand there; get her a tissue." So Mamma goes to find a tissue, and I'm just sitting there on the floor, wiping my nose with my hands and getting blood everywhere, and I realize my nose feels sort of weird and tight, like there's some strange pressure in there, and I just want some relief for it.

Finally Mamma comes back with some paper towels, and I start blowing my nose, even though Gramma Patty is trying to get me to tip my head back. As I'm blowing, I can feel something hard and solid in my nose, so I blow my nose again, and

I scrape at it with my finger, and a metal nail comes out and clatters onto the kitchen floor. A long, thin, rusty nail—must have been about two inches long. I heard Mamma screaming and Gramma Patty praying, but I was just staring at it there on the kitchen floor, fascinated that this thing had come out of me. And I sort of focused my mind and *pushed*, and a few more came out, one after another.

I thought I was done with this stuff, but apparently not.

I think I need to talk to Miss Pierre again.

MONDAY, APRIL 28, 2:34 P.M. (PRIVATE)

Mamma warned me against going back to Miss Pierre again, since Renee doesn't like it and she could use it as an excuse to send me away, but Renee isn't going to solve this problem. I don't know if anyone can, but at least Miss Pierre seems to understand what the hell we're dealing with.

Once Mamma and Gramma Patty left for work today, I looked up Miss Pierre's address and went to track her down. When I got to her house, my courage ran out and I realized it was kind of rude to just show up without calling ahead. I started to wonder if I should just walk back home and spend the day in bed, like I told Mamma I would, but the door wasn't closed, only the screen, and just as I was about to turn around, I heard Miss Pierre's voice: "Laetitia? Is that you? Well, come in here. Don't hover."

I wound up going in, and Miss Pierre didn't even seem surprised to see me. She just poured me a glass of lemonade and sat down at the table and asked what was troubling me. I told her all about what happened that morning, and she just sat there and nodded. I asked her, "Isn't there anything you can do for me? Something more than we've already done?"

Miss Pierre said yes, there were other steps we could take. She said she'd never done it before, but that she could perform an exorcism to get the demons out, if that's really what I wanted. But, she said, there wasn't any point unless I wanted to do it. That it wouldn't work if I didn't really want it. I must have given her such a look at that. How could I not want to fix this? Of course I want to! Whatever is going on is ruining my life. Why wouldn't I do anything in my power to get rid of it?

And Miss Pierre, calm as anything, said, "I don't know. Why don't you tell me?"

At first I didn't know what she was talking about, but then I thought about those pills, and how I keep not taking them, even though I know they were working. I didn't know what to say, though. How could I tell her? How could I admit to her that sometimes I don't want it to stop? Sometimes I lie awake, wondering what will come next, and almost wishing for it to come sooner. Sometimes it feels like I am out of control of my life and my body, and sometimes it feels like I have never been more in control, like there is all this power waiting for me, and all I have to do is reach out and grab it. I didn't know how to tell her any of that. I was scared she would judge me.

I couldn't tell her all of that, so I just fidgeted for a while and drank my lemonade. Then I sort of changed the subject, asking her something else I've been wondering. I don't understand why all this is happening to me and not someone else, so I asked if she knew what it was that made people susceptible to these kinds of attacks. But she wouldn't answer directly. Again, she turned it around and asked me what I thought. As if I'm the expert! I guess I was hoping she'd say something to reassure me, like maybe I'd come in contact with some possessed object, like a doll or a mirror. I've seen movies like that. Or maybe I could have caught it from someone, like a cold. Even if she said it was passed down from Mamma, that would be . . . better than the alternative.

Because the only other thing I can think of is that it's because of something wrong with me. I mean, demons don't affect *everyone* out there. They must have some reason for picking their targets. And if I can't think of anything else, then it must be because it sensed some kind of evil in me. I don't want to believe this, but how can I deny it? When I look back over my life, I was always convinced I was basically good. More than good—that I was *special*. ~Chosen~ by God Himself. What kind of person thinks that? I thought that just because I didn't steal or cuss or tell lies (much) and I went to church every week and sang praise songs in the choir, that meant I'd been touched by God's grace.

But what if it means just the opposite? Now I can see all that for what it really was: arrogance. Pride. Vanity. I didn't even really care about singing God's praises—I was much more interested in just using the church choir as training for my career as a pop diva. As soon as I couldn't do that, I lost all interest in church, and Mamma had to drag me there against my will. And my blog, which I thought was so full of inspiration—wasn't that really just another way of selling myself? Making myself look better than other people, making them jealous, to better hide the envy eating away at my own soul?

To regular people, I might have looked like a nice, sweet God-fearing girl with a bright future, but deep inside, how long have I known that my soul was twisted and corrupt, and I just refused to admit it? It probably wasn't very hard for the demons to see that in me, even if I hid it from regular people. And of course they would latch on to that and try to seize me as one of their own. How could I have any hope of fighting them off when my soul is already so crowded with darkness?

I tried to convey some of these thoughts to Miss Pierre, though it's hard to talk about them out loud. I was so afraid she was going to tell me I was already damned and beyond salvation, I was shaking as I tried to explain myself. But Miss Pierre . . . She didn't exactly disagree with me, but she did have another sort of perspective. She told me she's spent her whole life helping people afflicted with some kind of spirit or demon, and while she'd never seen a case as bad as mine before, she'd heard some stories from her *grand-mère*. What her *grand-mère* told her was that, in the worst cases, it usually means the person has been marked in some way. That they've been chosen for a special purpose. She told me a lot of saints, for example, have been visited by terrible visions, temptations, and possessions. It's considered a test of their faith, before they can move on to their true calling. She said the closer you get to God, the more vulnerable you become to darker influences.

It made sense when she said it. I don't know, though. That's a nice idea, but how could it apply to me? I'm just a normal teenager. I'm not "close to God" or anything. Looking back over my life, I've never been especially holy or righteous. It would be nice to believe that was my story, but it just doesn't make sense.

I asked Miss Pierre how people become saints, and she said they have to perform some miracles. That seemed out of my reach, unless you count Mamma saying it's a miracle when I clean my room without being asked three times. Miss Pierre said that's not what she had in mind. More like healing the sick or raising the dead.

That got my attention. I always thought raising the dead was considered black magic, but she said if Jesus did it, it must be okay. Then she laughed and said, "Why, you brought anyone back to life that I should know about?"

I thought about the bird and the rat. The rosebush and the unkillable mildew in my shower. All that stuff didn't feel like miracles at the time. A power that terrifying . . . I was sure it had to come from the Devil himself. But how does anyone ever know? How can I know what's God and what's the Devil and what's my own sick brain? And Miss Pierre said, "Honey, don't be so sure those aren't all the same thing." Which kind of shocked me. I mean, I can't imagine the pastor saying that *ever*. In fact, that seems like the kind of thinking he would specifically warn against. And suddenly it became clearer to me why most people in church avoid Miss Pierre. . . . That kind of thinking can get people into a lot of trouble.

But I let her go on, and she explained. God is all-powerful, right? I couldn't argue with that. But that means the Devil can only work with the powers God grants him. The Devil is part of God's plan and God's creation, and they are all bound up together. "Don't think of him as an enemy of God," she said. "Think of him as a tool. We're all tools of God, in the end."

I don't know what to think. It made sense to me, what she

was saying, but I don't know if it was wishful thinking. And if the Devil is on the same side as God, then I'm not sure I understand anything at all about the world anymore.

All I know is, I want all this stuff to stop and leave me alone. I want to have some peace again. And if an exorcism will do that, then that seems like the right answer. But Miss Pierre said I should think carefully about it. She said with the state I'm in, it could be a little like a fever. When you have a fever, it makes you feel terrible, and you can take some aspirin to bring the fever down, and it makes you feel better. But the fever isn't really the sickness—the fever is really your body's way of fighting off a deeper sickness that you might not even know is there. And bringing down the fever can be dangerous if it gets in the way of your body fixing itself.

I know what she means. Gramma Patty says this too: sometimes it's better to let the sickness run its course. Getting rid of the symptoms might make you feel better, but it could make you sicker in the long run. So I guess Miss Pierre is saying that all these symptoms I have—terrible thoughts and visions, and all these weird objects coming out of me—could be my body's way of fighting off something even worse. That's not exactly reassuring. And, as I pointed out to her, ignoring a fever can be dangerous too. People can die if they let the fever take over.

Miss Pierre didn't argue with that. She just told me to take some time and think it over.

MONDAY, APRIL 28, 9:10 P.M. (PRIVATE)

I just fixed up my altar, replaced some of the candles that had burned almost all the way down, and redid the salt barrier around the edge of my room. Then I just sat in bed for a while, and then I closed my eyes and tried to pray. This time it didn't feel like my voice was stuck, but it wasn't quite working. I knew all the words to say, but it was like talking on a telephone when the other person has hung up. I felt like none of my words went anywhere. I gave that up, and instead I tried to talk to God in my mind. I don't know if I even thought He was listening; I just wanted to put some thoughts out there into the universe. I told Him I believed in Him and I wanted to trust Him, but that it was difficult sometimes. And I have a lot of questions that maybe it's not my place to ask, but if He feels like giving answers, I'd sure appreciate it.

I still couldn't tell if that was doing any good, though, so that's why I got out my journal. My journal has been useful for helping figure some stuff out, so that's why I'm writing all this out.

I do feel a little better since my conversation with Miss Pierre. It's nice to be reminded that, no matter what bad things seem to be happening here, God is always in control. Maybe she's right and I need to just trust Him and see this through. But I do also have free will (I think), and I assume God wants me to use it. And what's going on is pretty terrifying. Maybe He wouldn't be too mad if I took the easy way out and got the exorcism. Just to get this thing out of me, whatever it is. I don't know. I'm not set on it yet. It's nice to know at least that there is a possible way out, but I'm not sure if I want to take that step. If God wants me to endure all this, then . . . well, I suppose I could take a little more.

But on the other hand, what if that whole idea is just that same old pride and arrogance? Who am I to think God has any kind of special plan for me? Maybe it's the demons themselves who want me to believe that so I make myself more vulnerable to them.

I wish there were some kind of sign to help me figure out if I'm making the right decision and should stick to this path, or if I should be more active in fighting off the forces tormenting me. But would I even know how to interpret a sign? At this point, how could I trust if it was from God or the devil or my own unconscious desires?

I don't know, but if I'm going to take Miss Pierre's advice and let this whole thing run its course, I guess I better prepare myself for it to get worse before it gets better.

TUESDAY, APRIL 29, 8:12 A.M. (PRIVATE)

I'm so scared; I don't know what to do. I need to write out what happened, to calm myself down and clear my thoughts.

When I went to bed last night, everything was reasonably normal and I was feeling okay after my talk with Miss Pierre, and now I don't even fully understand what happened.

Last I remember I was writing in my journal, and then I put it aside to think a little bit. I must have fallen asleep because then I remembered some kind of dream. It was actually the first good dream I remember having in a really long time, though I'm not sure of any details. Just an overwhelming sense of love and peace. But then it all shifted, and I felt that sharp, burning pain again in my side, which woke me up. For a few seconds I just lay there, staring up at the ceiling and trying to get my bearings. Then I realized the ceiling was a lot closer than I remembered it being. It was dark and I was still a little disoriented, so I tried to slowly turn my head and hoped that would make everything swing back to normal, but as I looked around the room, I caught sight of myself in the mirror across from my bed, and well, there's no other way to put this.

I was floating at least a couple of feet over my bed.

I just froze as terror seeped into every cell of my body. It's hard to describe that feeling when you suddenly realize everything you knew about the world, the rules of physics you thought were completely set in stone, mean nothing. In some sense, nothing that awful was happening, compared to other things I've experienced recently. I was just floating there. But it was way more terrifying because of the potential behind it— that knowledge that if this can happen, *anything* can happen, and there is no way to prepare or protect yourself.

Then I thought, *What if I'm dreaming?* I know I've had thoughts like that before, in the middle of a dream. That was a huge relief, but I still wanted to wake up as fast as possible, so I started screaming and thrashing to try to make myself wake up, but instead Mamma and Gramma Patty ran into the room. Mamma cried out and reached for me, tried to grab my pajamas and pull me back down, but Gramma Patty held her back and started praying in a loud, slow voice until Mamma joined in and they were both praying as hard as they could. Instead of being a comfort, every word was like a million needles under my skin, or like insects crawling on me, tiny animals burrowing into my body, flames burning me inside and out, and I felt like I was going to come apart. Then there was this massive noise, like a boom but also a ripping sound, like the air itself was being torn in two, and there was chaos everywhere and I felt the breath knocked out of me, so I couldn't scream anymore.

At some point I closed my eyes, so I opened them again and the room was filled with smoke. It took me a minute to realize the candles had gotten knocked over and set fire to the towel and the rug and some of the bedclothes. And all the glass in the room—the window, my mirrors, picture frames—had shattered. Mamma reached out to me, crying and begging me to take her hand and come toward her, until Gramma Patty appeared with the fire extinguisher from the kitchen and put out the fire.

That was a couple of hours ago. There's broken glass all over the floor of my room from the window and mirrors shattering, and the screens on my phone and laptop are smashed, though they both still turn on at least, which is good, since I can't exactly afford to replace them.

We've been cleaning ever since, trying to make the room livable again. And in that time, we've barely spoken. Only enough to get the work done. "The broom is in the hall closet" or "Fetch me the masking tape." That kind of thing. What else is there to say? What other response can there be to what happened?

I don't know what Mamma and Gramma Patty have in mind, but I can only think of one thing to do. I asked for a sign, and I sure as hell got one. We need to call Miss Pierre and arrange for the exorcism.

TUESDAY, APRIL 29, 3:12 P.M. (PRIVATE)

I wish I felt 100 percent sure about this exorcism. Even after everything that has happened, there's something that makes me hesitate to go through with it. I don't know if that's just ordinary nervousness, or whether there's a voice inside me that's warning against it. And if that's it, is it a trustworthy voice? Or an evil one?

In the meantime, we've been trying to clear up the mess in my room, but it's a huge chore, and I'm feeling pretty awful right now about everything I have brought on this house. I can't help wondering if Renee was right all along—that everyone would be better off if I were somewhere else, where I couldn't inflict this weird nightmare on them. If Mamma and Gramma Patty wind up hurt or cursed or something, and it was all my fault, I'd never be able to forgive myself. Maybe whatever this is, it's my problem, and they shouldn't have to deal with it.

But it doesn't even matter what I think, because I could never say any of this to Mamma. If I so much as hint at this idea, she only becomes all the more convinced that we all need to stay together, and she has to keep me close. If she's going to be like that, I guess that really leaves me no choice but to go through with the exorcism. Anything else is just too risky.

In any case, Miss Pierre is supposed to come tonight to help get this thing out of me once and for all. So ready or not, I'm going to have to face whatever this is.

WEDNESDAY, APRIL 30, 9:45 P.M. (PRIVATE)

Miss Pierre came over and did the exorcism tonight. It wasn't really what I'd been picturing. I guess all I know about exorcisms comes from movies, where a priest holds up a crucifix and says a bunch of stuff in Latin. But Miss Pierre isn't a priest, so I should have realized it wouldn't be quite like that.

She did bring a crucifix, but she also brought a chicken. A live one. That was strange in itself. . . . I'm not sure I'd ever seen a live chicken before! I mean, it's not like I've spent a lot of time on chicken farms. Chicken to me is something that comes battered and fried from a restaurant, or in featherless pieces from the supermarket. Not a real live bird with feathers and wings, squawking and carrying on in a cage.

I asked Miss Pierre what she was going to do with the chicken, and she said we were going to kill it. That almost gave me second thoughts. I mean, right at that moment, there wasn't anything bothering me. I felt fine. And I wasn't sure I wanted this chicken's blood on my hands. Metaphorically, and literally, too. Miss Pierre said we could call it quits if I'd changed my mind, but Mamma pointed out that I'm not a vegetarian, and I've never complained before about chickens getting killed so I can eat them. I asked if we were going to eat this one, but Miss Pierre said no. The whole point of the ritual is to get the bad spirits out of me and into the chicken so they can't harm anyone anymore. If we ate the chicken, that would give them another chance to get ahold on us, which makes sense in an odd sort of way. Anyway, I decided to put my ethical concerns aside and just go ahead with it. I was curious.

Miss Pierre made us all go out in the backyard, and she set up a bunch of candles and a big potful of water, and she started ripping up herbs and crushing them to release their oils. Then she dropped them into the water and mixed them around. She had a big rattle that she shook for a while, and she sang and chanted, too, but I couldn't understand any of it. It did have some effect on me though. I closed my eyes, and before I knew it, I was trembling so hard, I almost fell over. Mamma reached out and held me up, though.

The next thing I remember is Miss Pierre taking the chicken out of the cage, grabbing it by the feet, and dunking its head in the water. Then she pulled it back out and sort of waved it around a bunch. The weirdest thing was that the chicken didn't really react. . . . I expected it to struggle and squawk and beat its wings, but it just lay there, like it was hypnotized or something. She brought the chicken over to me, still chanting, and I had to will myself to stand still and not duck away when she rubbed it around my body and face. I think I cried out a few times. She brought it back to the pot and held it out with its head over the water. She took out a knife and scraped off some of the feathers, then cut the throat and let the blood run into the pot. She let it run out for a good long time, until the chicken was clearly dead, then she cut off the head and threw it into the pot and took the chicken inside to boil it. She said that way we'd know it was really completely dead.

That was pretty much it! So I guess it's all done now. Now we just wait and see if things get better.

WEDNESDAY, APRIL 30, 11:29 P.M. (PRIVATE)

I read over my entry about the exorcism just now, and I feel like I didn't necessarily tell the whole story. Everything I said did happen pretty much the way I described, but I didn't really talk much about what it felt like. And that's probably the most important part.

It was weird, really. Through the whole thing, I felt almost like I was two people—one Laetitia was standing there, watching this ceremony, curious about how the whole thing would play out, but basically detached. I saw myself close my eyes and start to shake, and I heard the strange sounds I was making as Miss Pierre brought the chicken near me. But none of it really touched me.

The other Laetitia . . . Well, I'm not sure exactly how to describe the other part. I remember, as soon as Miss Pierre started chanting, or maybe even before that with the smell of those herbs in the air as she was tearing them apart, that's when I felt a weird stirring deep inside me. Almost like a little animal in my chest or my stomach that was just waking up and turning around. And as Miss Pierre moved on to the singing and shaking her rattle, this feeling got stronger and spread around my whole body. That's when I started shaking, I think. At first it was just kind of a weird, squirmy feeling, like you might get after drinking too much coffee, but gradually it became more than that. I had this sense there was something inside of me that was fighting to get out. It didn't exactly hurt, but I felt like I might be split in two by this thing. And I just kept telling myself to relax, take deep breaths, and just let it happen. I didn't know if it would be painful or cause some kind of damage, but I knew it had to happen, so I tried to just let it. That's when I started trembling, and I stumbled a bit and sort of tripped over my own feet. I was so conscious of what was going on inside my body, I wasn't doing what I needed to do to keep myself upright.

The important thing, though, was it seemed to be working. I can't be sure it wasn't just my imagination, or wishful thinking, but I definitely *felt* something trying to work its way out of me. Almost like wiggling a loose tooth. But then it shifted. I could feel whatever it was starting to slip free from me and leave me behind, which was exactly the point, right? I had expected to feel relieved by this. To feel wholly myself again. But that's not what happened. Instead, as Miss Pierre sang and chanted and waved that chicken around, I just got this overwhelming sense of loss. Like it wasn't some foreign entity leaving me, but a piece of myself. I felt abandoned and empty, and I started to panic.

So at the last minute, just as Miss Pierre was starting to cut the chicken's throat, I sort of . . . held on. Not with my fingers or teeth or anything, but something inside of me. And I gripped on to that feeling with all my power, and it felt almost like I was *tugging* on that feeling with the strength of my soul, until I could feel whatever it was slipping back into me and filling me with this warm tingling fullness I never wanted to stop.

Then Miss Pierre cut off the chicken's head, and that sort of brought me back to myself. And I thought about how the whole point of this was that I was supposed to give up a piece of myself to this chicken. But I didn't. I kept it.

I'm worried now. This ritual was supposed to help put me back in control of my own body, and I'm not sure it did. I can't tell anymore who is in control—what part is me and what part is something else, or if in the end it's really all me and has been all along. I don't know what I might be capable of in this condition, and I'm wondering if it wouldn't be best if someone came around and cut *my* head off before I can become a danger to everyone around me.

Maybe I already am.

THURSDAY, MAY 1, 12:19 P.M. (PRIVATE)

Oh no, Renee is here! I forgot all about her, but now she's here for one of her unscheduled drop-in visits. I can hear her right now, talking to Mamma in the kitchen. Maybe if I go down and act totally normal, she won't bother to come in here and see what a mess my room still is. We never really got it back into shape after the night of the fire. I think we were all so focused on whatever is wrong with me, trying to fix it, we didn't worry about the room so much. But if Renee sees it like this, it's going to be really obvious this isn't exactly a "stable environment." This is exactly the kind of excuse she's been looking for to send me away.

Maybe she won't notice. Or she'll cut us some slack. I've swept up all the glass, I think, but there's cardboard over the window and burn marks on the walls, and she is definitely going to have questions about both. This is exactly the kind of thing she was worried about, and I'm afraid if she sees the room, she'll have me sent away to go live with strangers again. I don't want that. I'm so scared.

I need to pull myself together. I need to go into the kitchen and talk to her and reassure her that everything is okay.

CHILD REMOVED INTO EMERGENCY PROTECTIVE CUSTODY WITHOUT COURT ORDER:
REPORT AND JUSTIFICATION

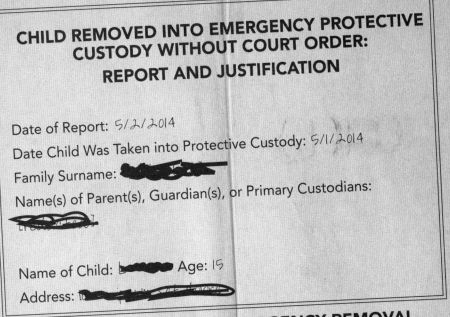

Date of Report: 5/2/2014

Date Child Was Taken into Protective Custody: 5/1/2014

Family Surname: ▬▬▬

Name(s) of Parent(s), Guardian(s), or Primary Custodians:

▬▬▬

Name of Child: ▬▬▬ Age: 15

Address: ▬▬▬

JUSTIFICATION FOR EMERGENCY REMOVAL (CHOOSE AS MANY AS APPLY):

☒ The child's physical or mental health is in severe and imminent danger due to inability, refusal, or neglect on the part of parent(s), legal guardian(s), or other custodian(s) to provide adequate shelter, nutrition, clothing, education, medical care, or supervision.

☒ The child's parent(s), legal guardian(s), or other custodian(s) appear to have physically or mentally injured the child by act or inaction.

☐ There is compelling evidence of child sexual abuse.

☐ The child's physical or mental health has been endangered due to the parent(s), legal guardian(s), or other custodian(s) employing the child in a form of illegal or inappropriate labor.

☒ The child has significantly endangered his or her own well-being or the well-being of others.

DESCRIBE THE CIRCUMSTANCES THAT LED TO THE REMOVAL OF THE CHILD INTO PROTECTIVE CUSTODY:

On Thursday, May 1, I arrived at the ~~████~~ residence for an impromptu well check, primarily to see if █ was keeping up with her medication schedule, and also to check more generally on the welfare of the ~~███~~ family. █ met me at the door and invited me into the kitchen, where █ (C's mother, █'s grandmother) already was. I asked █ how █ was adjusting to her medication, but █ was mostly nonresponsive, and seemed not to have made any effort to ensure █ took her pills on schedule, even though she had agreed to support this treatment plan last time we spoke.

When pressed, █ insisted medication would not

solve the "real" problem in the house, and could only cover it up. She continued to put forward the idea that a demonic force was threatening ▬ and the whole family, and it would only be removed by God's will. The discussion between us became animated. Voices were raised, at which point ▬ came out of her room and into the kitchen. I deescalated the argument and asked ▬ to tell me in her own words whether she was taking her medication regularly, and how she was adjusting to it. She insisted—as she had last time—that she was taking everything according to the schedule and having no ill effects. She asked then if we could go out to the diner and get a slice of pie, as had been our tradition until recently.

I was about to agree, but I sensed something furtive in the way she was speaking, as if she wanted to distract me from something, so I asked if we could speak in her room instead. She refused at first, which led me to conduct a more thorough investigation of the rest of the house. It was at that time that I discovered traces of what appeared to be blood in the yard and on the back stairs. At first all three residents denied any knowledge of where it came from, but when I demanded to know if anyone had been hurt, C▬ confessed that a local voodoo practitioner had come and performed an animal sacrifice to rid ▬ of her demonic entity. This was explicitly contrary to the plan we had agreed to earlier, in which C▬ would cease to have any contact with this traditional healer/folk practitioner and would contact me first if she had any problem that needed to be resolved.

At this point, I entered ▬'s room and discovered it had been badly damaged: there were burn marks on the wall and floor, and the window was broken and had been covered with a piece of cardboard. No one would explain exactly what had happened, but I surmised it was the result of ▬ leaving lit candles unattended—which she had promised me she would not do—as part of an "altar" to ward off evil spirits.

I made the decision that ▬ could not be left safely in her current situation, and began the process for an emergency removal. I contacted my supervisor, who gave me verbal approval to bring ▬ into temporary state custody until a stable environment for her—either with her mother or elsewhere—could be established. I asked ▬ to come with me willingly, and when she refused, I contacted the police to come aid in ▬'s removal.

Two police officers arrived a few minutes later,

tongues"), walked and moved in a strange manner, and jumped and scrambled around the room with unusual energy.

By the time the ambulance arrived, L— appeared to have worn herself out, and she collapsed in the middle of the room, moaning and rocking. She put up no further physical resistance, and was taken directly to the psychiatric wing of ▆▆ Hospital.

PROVIDE JUSTIFICATION FOR WHY EMERGENCY REMOVAL WAS INDICATED:

Upon surveying the situation at the ▆▆ house that afternoon, I came to the unavoidable conclusion that L— provided an immediate danger to herself and others. Additionally, there was significant evidence that L—'s custodial parent was not capable of adequately providing for L—. L— has been frequently truant from school in the past few months, as well as unduly influenced by her mother's fixation on demons as an explanation for any negative event in their lives. Everyone in the household has been secretive and uncooperative, and they have failed to abide by the agreed-to guidelines. It is not a healthy environment for L—

Officer D— and Officer B—. L— was crouched in a corner, facing the wall and rocking slightly while repeating that she didn't want to leave. One of the police officers approached and touched her gently on the shoulder. L— spun around, growled, and bared her teeth at the officer. Both officers backed away, and I approached again and tried to reason with L—. I explained that the removal was only temporary, that if she was compliant, the situation could be resolved more quickly, and I assured her I would do everything in my power to make sure she was back at home with her family as soon as possible. This seemed to calm her down at first, but when I tried to coax her outside, she returned to hissing and spitting. Officer B— tried to grab her from behind, but she sank her teeth into his hand, and when Officer D— tried to intervene, she clawed out a chunk from his left cheek and pressed it into her mouth.

L— was completely out of control, and I was worried the police officers would be compelled to use deadly force on her. I asked them to back away from her and leave her alone, and they called for an ambulance and more backup. While we waited for the ambulance to arrive, L— continued to behave strangely, though somewhat less aggressively: she appeared to engage in glossolalia ("speaking in

EXCERPT FROM OFFICIAL POLICE REPORT:
OFFICER D████'S REPORT
REPORT DATE: 5/1/2014

WE RECEIVED A CALL AT APPROXIMATELY 18:20 ON THURSDAY, MAY 1, TO ASSIST SOCIAL SERVICES WITH A DOMESTIC SITUATION AT [ADDRESS REDACTED]. WE ARRIVED AT [ADDRESS REDACTED] AT 18:26 AND KNOCKED ON THE FRONT DOOR. THE GRANDMOTHER LET US IN AND SHOWED US TO THE ROOM WHERE R. S., THE SOCIAL SERVICES WORKER, WAS TRYING TO REASON WITH AN ADOLESCENT FEMALE, ██. R. S. INDICATED SHE HAD DETERMINED IT NECESSARY TO REMOVE ██ FROM THE HOUSEHOLD IMMEDIATELY FOR HER OWN SAFETY AND THE SAFETY OF OTHERS, BUT ██ WAS RESISTING.

I STEPPED FORWARD AND ASKED ██ TO COME PEACEFULLY WITH US. SHE WAS UNRESPONSIVE, SO I PUT A HAND ON HER SHOULDER. ██ REACTED SUDDENLY, SPINNING AROUND AND SNAPPING AND SNARLING AT ME LIKE A RABID DOG. I STEPPED AWAY FROM HER TO REEVALUATE THE SITUATION. R. S. TRIED TO TALK TO HER AGAIN, BUT SHE DID NOT RESPOND, AND DID NOT SEEM TO HEAR HER. IT WAS AS IF SHE HAD TURNED INTO SOME KIND

OF WILD ANIMAL. SHE HAD MOVED AWAY FROM THE CORNER, SO OFFICER B███ WENT TO RESTRAIN HER FROM BEHIND. L███ GAVE A HOWL AND BIT INTO HIS HAND, THEN TURNED ON ME. I WAS TRYING TO GET HER OFF MY FELLOW OFFICER WHEN SHE LUNGED TOWARD ME AND SCRATCHED AT MY FACE, GOUGING OUT A DEEP GASH. I PULLED MY WEAPON AND TOLD HER TO PUT HER HANDS ON HER HEAD. INSTEAD SHE CALMLY LICKED THE BLOOD FROM HER FINGERS.

I KEPT MY WEAPON TRAINED ON HER AS OFFICER B███ CALLED IN FOR MORE BACKUP. THAT'S WHEN L███ STOOD UP STRAIGHT FOR THE FIRST TIME AND ADVANCED SLOWLY TOWARD ME, EVEN THOUGH I STILL HAD MY WEAPON AIMED AT HER AND WAS ORDERING HER TO STOP. SHE IGNORED MY INSTRUCTIONS AND BEGAN SPEAKING IN A WEIRD INHUMAN VOICE. I DIDN'T BELIEVE A VOICE LIKE THAT COULD COME OUT OF AN ADOLESCENT FEMALE. I DIDN'T RECOGNIZE THE LANGUAGE, BUT IT MAY HAVE BEEN LATIN.

THEN SHE SUDDENLY CROUCHED DOWN FOR A MOMENT AND STARTED MOVING BACKWARD ACROSS THE ROOM USING WEIRD JERKING MOVEMENTS, AS IF HER BONES WERE POPPING OUT OF THEIR JOINTS. I THOUGHT ONCE SHE REACHED

THE WALL BEHIND HER, SHE WOULD BE FORCED
TO STOP, BUT SHE DIDN'T. SHE KEPT MOVING UP
THE SIDE OF THE WALL. I DON'T KNOW HOW SHE
WAS DOING IT. IT DID NOT SEEM TO BE HUMANLY
POSSIBLE.

WHEN SHE REACHED THE CEILING, SHE LET
OUT A SHRIEK AND FLIPPED OVER, LANDING ON HER
BACK ON THE FLOOR, STILL HISSING AND SPITTING.
OFFICER B▬ LEFT THE ROOM WHILE R. S. AND I
MOVED TO RESTRAIN HER. SHE THRASHED FOR
A COUPLE OF MINUTES, BUT BY THE TIME THE
AMBULANCE ARRIVED, SHE WAS PASSIVE, THOUGH
STILL NOT COOPERATIVE. THE EMTS LOADED HER
ONTO A STRETCHER AND TOOK HER INTO THE
AMBULANCE.

I've served on the ████ police force for thirteen years, and six years before that in ████, and in all my experience I have never seen anything like this before. A teenage girl as strong as two trained law officers, who walks up walls and curses at you in weird languages? I'm not an expert in these things, but that's not normal.

Officer D~ and I were totally unprepared for the situation we walked into. I understood we had a noncooperative fifteen-year-old female who needed to be brought into custody, and when we got there, that's what it looked like. She was crouched in the corner, crying, but as soon as she turned around, there was something in her eyes that made me cold. It wasn't human. And she was biting and barking like a mad dog, and she caught me by the hand and bit me. It was a severe bite. I had to go to the emergency room. Officer D~ was trying to control her, and she scratched his face.

I've never seen anything like it. I was terrified, and I made the decision to radio for more backup. While I was talking to the dispatcher, I heard a voice speaking some strange language, but it definitely didn't sound like a teenage girl's voice. And it didn't sound like English—maybe Russian? Or German. I don't know. When I heard that, I turned to look, and she was running backward up the wall. Even in the Olympics, they can't do that. Then she jumped off and fell to the floor.

I had to leave the room after that. I had no idea what she might do next. I just thought, This isn't a situation for the police. This girl needs a priest.

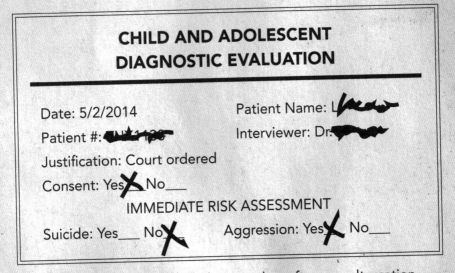

CHILD AND ADOLESCENT DIAGNOSTIC EVALUATION

Date: 5/2/2014   Patient Name: L~~eow~~

Patient #: ~~████████~~   Interviewer: Dr. ~~████~~

Justification: Court ordered

Consent: Yes X̶ No___

IMMEDIATE RISK ASSESSMENT

Suicide: Yes___ No X̶   Aggression: Yes X̶ No___

Patient was admitted yesterday after an altercation with police. Patient was unconscious upon admittance. Patient regained full consciousness this morning, and was examined for diagnostic purposes this afternoon. Initial diagnosis of schizoaffective disorder may need to be revisited. Patient admits to delusions and hallucinations, but her described hallucinations are sufficiently atypical, as to render diagnosis difficult. Patient also appears to be an accomplished liar, and therefore her descriptions of her own symptoms must be treated with an appropriate degree of skepticism.

Patient claims no memory of the event that resulted in her hospital admission, nor any memory of previous similar events. Again, her symptoms are markedly atypical for amnesia resulting from physical or psychological trauma.

Evidence from the patient's file suggests an alternative

diagnosis: possibly folie à deux, or a form of shared delusion with another person, in this case, her mother. As is typical of such scenarios, the mother's stronger personality has overwhelmed the daughter's weaker one, until the patient is forced to modify her entire conception of the world to fit her mother's various delusions. In this case, the mother has shown a persistent belief (going back at least twelve years) in the presence of demons and malevolent spirits in her life, affecting every aspect of her and her family's existence.

During analysis, the patient described a very intense relationship with her mother that may exhibit features of codependency. The patient may have unconsciously determined that love, attention, and support would only be granted to her in this household as long as she supported and participated in her mother's delusions.

As yet, there is no conclusive evidence of sexual, physical, or emotional abuse or other latent trauma, but it would be unwise to rule out any or all at this stage.

RECOMMENDATION:

Patient should remain in hospital care, under close observation, until her physical and psychological states can be stabilized. It may be necessary to keep her separate from her mother for an extended period of time in order for the shared delusions to dissipate and the patient to become more cooperative. Though every effort must be made to reunite this family, it is likely that this patient will ultimately fair better in a foster care environment.

If, however, the mother seeks treatment for her own delusions and successfully overcomes them, this recommendation may be reconsidered.

MEDICATION:

Patient was previously prescribed a course of antipsychotic medication, but that treatment plan needs to be reconsidered in light of an updated diagnosis. The current treatment plan emphasizes daily therapeutic sessions with the attending psychiatrist, plus group therapy sessions (contingent on the patient remaining nonviolent). Low-dose sedatives are also indicated until the staff can be sure the patient is not a danger to herself or others.

TUESDAY, MAY 6, 2:59 P.M. (PRIVATE)

I have my laptop back! It feels like it's been ages since I updated here, but I guess it hasn't been that long. It just feels like a long time because a lot has happened. I don't really remember too much—all I know for sure is, Renee showed up at the house on a surprise visit, asked about the damage to my room, she and Mamma started arguing, and I . . . I don't know. Sometime later I came to in this hospital bed. Everything in between is kind of a blur.

I was really confused and upset when I woke up here, strapped down and surrounded by strangers. And for the first few days no one would tell me anything. They just hooked me up to machines and fed me pills, and sometimes they let me out of bed to meet with a psychiatrist, but that was about answering *his* questions. He wasn't at all interested in answering mine.

He won't tell me anything definite, just that I had some kind of "episode," and keeps prodding me again and again to tell him everything I remember. I keep saying there's isn't anything! He knows what happened a lot better than I do. It's all a blank to me. I really don't see the point of going over it again and again when there's nothing to go over.

But now finally they've let Gramma Patty come to see me, and let her bring me some of my stuff, including my phone and my laptop. (The screens are still cracked, but I can see what I'm typing, for the most part.) She brought me clothes, too, but no belts, and they took all the shoelaces out of my shoes. And they've banned all my wigs and makeup, for some reason. It would take a more ingenious brain than mine to figure out how to kill myself with a bright pink wig and sparkly eye shadow. They won't even let me have my bandannas and scarves, which seems really cruel. Without at least those, I feel naked. Like a sick person.

Which maybe I am.

Gramma Patty has told me *some* stuff the doctors and nurses wouldn't. Though as usual, she begs off and says she doesn't like talking about this stuff, as if she thinks it's somehow dangerous to even tell me what happened. She did say that when Renee saw the condition of my room and heard some of what Mamma had to say about it, she decided I needed to be removed from the house then and there. Renee asked me to come with her, but I didn't want to go, so she wound up calling the police, and eventually an ambulance. Gramma Patty says it took four full-grown men to wrestle me into the ambulance. I really can't picture that. I'm not a big girl.

I thought about this awhile, and then I asked her, "Was I

violent? Did I hurt anyone?" She didn't answer right away, and when she did, she just patted my hand and smiled and told me not to worry. Said everyone was going to be fine. I guess that means I did hurt someone, maybe more than one person, and I have no idea what I did or how bad it was.

I'm kind of afraid to ask for more details. I'm not sure I want to know what really happened. In a way, I'm glad I don't remember it.

Whatever that was back there, who hurt those people, it wasn't me.

THURSDAY, MAY 8, 12:50 P.M. (PRIVATE)

Gramma Patty visited again today. It is so good to see a familiar face in the middle of this nightmare, even if it's only for a few minutes at a time. I miss my mamma, though. Gramma Patty told me Mamma isn't allowed to come see me yet, but she'll come as soon as she can. Renee and some other people from social services have given her a list of things she needs to do to prove she can provide me with a stable home. Gramma Patty says they are working together to get it done as quickly as possible, but there's no way to rush these things.

I asked her if I could come home right away, once Mamma has done everything she needs to do. She said no. There's some stuff I need to do too. I have to convince the doctors here that I'm better, and that I can be trusted not to have another episode or throw any fits. I wish I could trust *myself* about that. But I think Gramma Patty's message was pretty clear: whatever I think might be going on inside of me, if I want to go home, I better figure out what the doctors want to hear and say it.

FRIDAY, MAY 9, 10:43 A.M. (PRIVATE)

Holy Jesus, I don't know what's happening. Am I awake or am I dreaming?

I was just reading over my last couple of entries and something weird happened. They looked strange to me. The screen started to swim in front of my eyes, like I had gotten some dirt in them, and I was tearing up, but I blinked and rubbed them and it didn't go away. Instead the screen was rolling and rippling and buckling right before my eyes. I thought I had to be hallucinating and that it was a trick of my eyes or my brain and not actually on the screen itself. So I took some screen caps to reassure myself, and look:

I just went back and looked again, and the entries themselves look normal to me now. But the screen caps are still messed up!

Oh God, I just noticed something else, too. Those aren't the words I originally wrote. Mostly it is, but in the bubbled parts, there are other words that weren't part of the original post.

I guess. Which is weird, I know. Why should I feel guilty? I wasn't on the jury, I didn't shoot Dwayne Robinson. REMEMBER What does any of it have to do with me? How could I possibly have inf_____ _____. Which is weird, I know _____ guilty? I wasn't on the jur___ _____ne Robinson. What does _____ ____ to do with me? How could I possibl_____ _____ed the decision of a bunch of jury members I've never even met? But for some reason I feel like I should have done more, I should have gone to those demonstrations, I should have prayed.

But I couldn't. I guess that's what's freaking me out a little. Just before they made the announcement, Mamma suggested we all join hands and _____ LIAR Gramma Patty asked me to lead the prayer, and I couldn't. I s____ _____ about halfway through when my throat closed up and no sound came out. It wa___ _____ singing when this all started. Only it was SAVE US ___ ___ ____ It wasn't just that my voice died... my mind went blank too. I was only repe_____ _____ said thousands of times in my life, but somehow standing there in front o___ ____ ___ reporter saying they'd have the verdict in just a minute, my brain just emptie____ _____ ___ouldn't go on.

So I just looked up and stared at SACRIFICE Gramma Patty and Mamma like an idiot. And Gramma Patty saw and just squeezed my hand a little and then she took over and finished the prayer and it was fine. I felt relieved, like she'd saved it, and nothing really bad had happened. I just chalked it up to nerves about the trial, and being overexcited.

But then the announcement came and how could I avoid thinking about what had

REMEMBER

LIAR

SAVE US

SACRIFICE

Where the hell did they come from? And what do they mean? I don't understand why this is happening.

TUESDAY, MAY 13, 6:23 A.M. (PRIVATE)

I've been wanting to write in here, but I kept holding back because I didn't know what to say. I think it's time I admit to myself what's going on here. It's time to face all the things I keep denying.

There are things I know. I didn't want to write them down because I was afraid that would make them real, but they are real, and I can't hide from them anymore.

Those words that appeared in my journal . . . *Remember* . . . *Liar* . . . I said I had no idea what they meant, but I do know. They're talking to me. Because I am a liar. And I do remember.

What I said before was all lies. What I told the doctors, and Gramma Patty, and even this journal. I said I didn't remember anything from my "episode," and my attack on those cops, but the truth is, I knew just what I was doing. I knew what I was doing, and I liked it.

I've been lying to everyone this whole time, and even to myself. That's what people always do, isn't it? When they've done something terrible, and people ask them about it? They always say, one minute we were arguing, and the next thing I knew he was dead and the gun was in my hand. I must have blacked out the rest.

It's easier that way, and it's what people want to hear. They think they want to hear what you were thinking, what it felt like, but they don't. It's too horrible. They'd turn away from you if they knew, and call you a monster. So instead you give them the same old script: *I blacked out. It's like something took over my body. I don't remember a thing.* That way, you get to still be human.

But now I know what a lie that is. I do remember. I remember the whole thing as clear as anything. I remember Mamma and Renee arguing, and I was trying to calm everyone down, and Renee said she had no choice; she had to get me out of this house. And I heard Mamma crying as Renee reached out a hand to me to take me away, and I felt this wave of anger and fear surge up in me, so I bared my teeth, and all my emotions came out of me in the form of a terrible, inhuman noise. I remember it all—cursing and spitting, biting that policeman, and even running up the wall. But it's almost like remembering a movie or a dream, because even as I was conscious of all those things, my attention was so much more focused on what was going on inside of me. And what was inside me was a rage so dark and thick, it seemed to fill me up, to replace my blood. It was like a black cloud, so heavy I felt almost like I could explode with it

284

and send burning bile raining down over this whole city.

Although that's not quite right either. I'm trying to find words that fit, but something in me keeps wanting to phrase it so it sounds like some outside force that took over my body. So I can point to this or that and say, see? That's clearly not me. That's the demon. But the truth is, that's not how it felt at the time. At the time, there was no line separating me from the other, evil thing. There was only me all the way through. And that rage and evil were built out of every bad thing I've done or every wicked thought I've had throughout my whole life.

I'm not okay. I think I've known this for a long time, but I didn't want to face it. I came closest when I was talking to Miss Pierre, and she was trying to convince me that all this was happening to me because God chose me, but I knew even then that wasn't true. This whole idea of a demon possessing me . . . I don't think I ever *really* believed it. It's a nice story that makes me look like the good guy or like a victim. Like I was just some innocent who got attacked by evil out of bad luck.

But that was just a lie I told myself and everyone else to hide what's really going on. There isn't anything good in me, and there never was. Everything I have ever done on this earth has been in service not to God, but to my own glory and vanity and pride. To the Beast. If there is any demon, it's not possessing me. . . . It *is* me.

TUESDAY, MAY 13, 4:26 P.M. (PRIVATE)

My doctor here is "unhappy with my progress." I didn't tell him anything about what happened with the journal entries, or that I remember anything about my attack, but it's his job to get inside my head. I guess he can tell I'm hiding something. He seems to think I'm more in danger than ever.

Of course he can't know what's really going on, but in his way, he's probably more right about the danger—to myself and to everyone around me—than he even understands. He thinks this is some kind of mental illness, and if he can just find the right combination of pills, he can fix me up and I'll go back to being "normal." What he hasn't figured out is that this *is* my normal. There's no outside force, and there's no disease I've picked up. It's all the darkness that was always in me, just finally rising to the surface.

The only thing that's really changed is that I used to be able to control it better. I had all this wickedness and hate and anger and jealousy in me, but I was careful never to let it show. But now it's all just bleeding out of me, taking over my life. The visions I experienced, and the nails and bones and such that come out of me are just physical versions of the ugly thoughts and impulses that have always been there. The only thing that scares me now is what will happen if this process is allowed to go any further. What damage will I wind up doing once they let me out and there are no walls or straps or sedatives to stop me?

Maybe Miss Pierre or Mamma would say God could stop me, but I guess I don't believe it anymore. If God were real and good, He would have stopped me long ago. The fact that He hasn't just proves this world and whoever is running it is completely fucked.

But at least I still have some control. I think I finally understand what all those visions and dreams were. All the torture I was forced to see and experience. They were the tortures of Hell, and the visions were a message telling me where I belong. I fought it as long as I could, but it's the only answer that makes sense. The sooner I give in and accept my destiny, the safer everyone will be from me.

No one else is going to stop me, but maybe I can stop myself before I do any more damage.

INCIDENT REPORT

Patient # ███████

Patient Last Name: J██████

Patient First Name: L████████

Date of Incident: 5/14/2014

Approximate Time of Incident: 3:15 a.m.

Date of Report: 5/14/2014

After steady improvement over the last couple of weeks, the patient has regressed suddenly and dramatically.

Between three and four a.m. last night, an orderly making rounds notified the night nurse that loud noises were coming from the patient's room. The nurse notified the doctor on call, and proceeded to gather another nurse and orderly to assess the situation. Inside the room, they discovered that the patient had torn the metal bars free from the window casing, and was in the process of hurling herself at the glass. The glass panes are of double thickness and designed to be shatterproof, but even so, upon examination, the patient had clearly managed to damage the glass by repeated extreme force directed at the same spot. Lacking any blunt object in the room, the patient appeared to have used her own head to accomplish this.

For the next hour the nurse and orderlies tried to subdue the patient without much success. The orderlies both suffered deep lacerations to their faces, and the nurse suffered a broken wrist and three broken fingers. Eventually the patient exhausted herself, and a strong sedative was administered. The patient was then put to bed under heavy restraints.

It was only at this point that the nurse became aware of the blood, which was coming not only from the patient's head, and now from the orderlies' faces, but also from the patient's own wrists and mouth. The doctor on call arrived to perform an examination, and determined that the patient had chewed through the skin, veins, and tendons on both her wrists in an apparent suicide attempt. This process had also done considerable damage to her mouth: at one point during the examination, the doctor discovered a tooth lodged in the bones of the patient's wrist. A dental examination confirmed that this was her own tooth, ripped free by the exertion of her self-inflicted violence.

Although the patient was already unconscious, the doctor chose to increase the strength of the sedative being used on her.

CONCLUSION: Patient appears to be suffering from a critical level of suicidal ideation. She will stop at nothing, it seems, to achieve her goal of self-annihilation. She currently poses a severe danger to herself and others. It is difficult to say whether this condition was brought on by psychological factors or organic factors, possibly including a negative reaction to medication.

RECOMMENDATION: Restraints and heavy sedation until the patient is calm enough to engage in therapeutic treatment again.

Patient Notes, Dr. ██████████

Date: 5/16/2014

Patient #██████████

Patient Last Name: J████

Patient First Name: L████████

    Patient is being maintained under heavy sedation and has not awoken since the incident. I would like to begin reducing the level of sedation so a psychiatric examination can be performed, but I am mindful of the orderlies and nursing staff, who appear nervous around the patient even when she is under heavy physical restraints. This is understandable, given the near superhuman strength she exhibited, necessary to pry the iron bars off the window. As yet, there has been no satisfactory explanation for how the patient was able to do this.

    Nevertheless, tomorrow I would like to begin experimentally lowering the sedative enough to allow her to awaken. We cannot maintain her in this state indefinitely. This is an unusual case, so I am waiting on consults from colleagues before I make a definitive decision.

Patient Notes, Dr. ████████████

Date: 5/16/2014

Patient # ██████████████

Patient Last Name: J████

Patient First Name: L████████

    After affirmative consultation with Drs. ████████ and ██████, the process has been initiated to reduce the sedative and encourage the patient slowly and carefully back to consciousness. So far the patient is nonresponsive, but she is still under quite heavy sedation for someone her age and size. I will cut the dose again.

Patient Notes, Dr. ████████████

Date: 5/19/2014

Patient #████████████

Patient Last Name: J████████

Patient First Name: L████████████

    Patient remains nonresponsive, even after considerable reduction in the sedative. I am growing concerned that some permanent damage may have been done to her brain as a result of overmedication by the doctor on call. This is in addition to the probable severe head trauma the patient inflicted on herself during her incident. I will order a brain scan for the patient tomorrow.

Patient Notes, Dr. ████████████
Date: 5/20/2014
Patient # ██████████
Patient Last Name: J███
Patient First Name: L███████

The results of the brain scan are not at all what I expected. The scan showed unusual hyperactivity in the patient's brain—not decreased metabolism, as would be expected from a traumatic brain injury or drug overdose, but heightened activity all over, even in normally dormant areas. Nevertheless, the patient remains unconscious. This is a very curious and surprising result. I may need another consult.

I've always thought so. I hate going down there to do laundry, and I am sure that's why. That's where the bad spirits are coming from. I think something terrible must have happened down there, like a murder or a black magic ritual. Now I just need proof. There's a dirt floor, and if we dig around, I'm sure we'll find some evidence. I convinced one of those officers to come over and investigate, and when we find it, no one will be able to call me a liar ever again.

So you see? Mamma has the whole situation under control. Don't worry about a thing except getting good and healthy, and when you wake up, you'll be able to come straight home.

Love,
Mamma

what everyone knows is true. And they tell me the only way I can have my baby back home is if I say we made everything up. How is that going to solve anything? How is that going to help next time a demon comes around? It just makes us more vulnerable.

But don't worry; your mamma has an idea. I've been thinking about why we are experiencing these trials, and there has to be something inside the house that has brought all this on us. Some kind of cursed object or a portal that all the demons are traveling through. I learned about it on this TV show all about haunted places and possessions. If I can just find some evidence of that, some hard proof no one can disagree with, they'll all have to admit I was right all along, and someone will help us close the portal. We'll finally have peace. And then they'll let you come home.

I was going to call up those people from TV to come investigate, but their answering service said they were busy with other folks. But with God, anything is possible, so I prayed and prayed about it, asking God to show me where the demons were coming from, and the other day I got this feeling. You know all about my feelings, and how I have learned to trust them. And I'm just about convinced that what we're looking for is in the basement. You know I have never liked those basement stairs. They are downright creepy, and

Letter from Ms. J███████ to L███████
Friday, May 23, 2014
(transcribed from handwritten letter)

Dear Laetitia,

I'm so worried about you, baby. It kills me that they won't even let me into see you, but they say it's too dangerous right now, with the fever you're running. But with all those doctors fussing over you, I can't help thinking you're bound to get better soon. I know you'll do it for me. You wouldn't leave your mamma all alone. Gramma Patty and I pray every day for you to recover and come home to us.

We are still working on getting things set up so you can live with us again. It just drives me crazy, because after all we've been through together, and then what happened when Renee was here, it really gets to me that no one will believe me as to what's really going on. There were witnesses! Renee and those police officers—how much more reliable can witnesses be? And those police officers will tell you what happened, how they saw with their own eyes how this family is being tormented by the Devil.

But still, social services insists I'm the one at fault; I'm the crazy one. Even though I'm just telling them

Patient Notes, Dr. ███████████

Date: 5/21/2014

Patient #███████████

Patient Last Name: J████

Patient First Name: L█████████

Some improvement today, in that the patient showed signs of increasing consciousness. Her eyelids fluttered repeatedly, and she attempted to speak at one point, though her words were unintelligible. However, it appears the patient has now developed a dangerously high fever that is so far resistant to drugs.

Tuesday, May 27
(Transcribed from Crayon and Paper)

Finally they are letting me write again, though they won't let me have my laptop back until I can prove I'm not going to freak out again. I'm not, but I understand why they're afraid. I would be too. But I'm not like I was back then. I'm the same person, but I understand things better now.

They must have sedated me pretty hardcore, because I don't remember anything from those first couple of days but bad dreams. Then I started to wake up a little more and feel more conscious and aware, but I was still miserable and just wanted to get away from myself, from this world, from my body. I was too drugged up to do anything, but I still had all those despairing thoughts from that last incident, and I was almost dreading having to deal with normal human life again. And I was tired of seeing the same old doctors and nurses and orderlies come through my room.

I spent every day wishing Mamma or Gramma Patty would come visit me, just to see a familiar face, but I guess they weren't allowed. But there was this one woman who came every day and sat with me for hours. She's a nun, I think, from the way she was dressed. It's a Catholic hospital, so I guess they let the nuns visit with the patients sometimes. She's old, older than Gramma Patty, but she has a very sweet face, and just knowing she was sitting there, watching as I drifted in and out of sleep, made me feel better than all the doctors and psychiatrists and nurses put together.

She never said anything that I can remember. I don't even know her name. I wonder if she's taken a vow of silence. Up to that point, I'd been feeling so abandoned. After I saw those messages in my journal, I felt like everything was telling me there was something evil in me. Either something had taken over my soul, or maybe it had been dormant in my soul all along and had just been reawakened. And all I could think was that God would never accept someone as tainted and evil as me, so I was alone in the universe. I thought, if my soul was going to get sucked down to Hell, then so much the better because that would be where it belonged.

But if a nun is still willing to sit with me and hold my hand and pray over me, I can't be all bad, can I? It made me think there might still be hope.

Today before she left, she put a rosary in my hand. I don't think I've ever seen one before, except in movies and on TV. I know Gramma Patty would say that's all superstitious nonsense. She explained once that they're for counting out your prayers, but in our church, we don't pray like that, repeating the same words over and over. She said we speak from the heart as the spirit moves us. Still, I'm glad to have it. It's pretty, and it's nice to know someone hasn't given up on me.

WEDNESDAY, MAY 28
(TRANSCRIBED FROM PENCIL AND PAPER)

I slept through the visit from the nun today. Disappointing, because I've started looking forward to seeing her every day. But I know she was there because my dreams are always calmer when she's sitting by me. Sometimes she rests a hand on my forehead, and I get this peaceful feeling, like being a kid again and knowing people will take care of me and I have nothing to worry about. I haven't felt that in so long, and today, even in my dreams, I could feel it.

When I woke up, there was a new plant sitting on the table. I don't know what it is, but I took a picture of it. It's kind of strange. It doesn't have any flowers, just leaves. I wonder where she even got it. Still, I kind of like it. It makes the room feel less dreary.

I just asked one of the nurses, and I guess it's a palm leaf.

That makes sense—I guess it does look like it came off a palm tree. Not that I've ever seen a palm tree in real life. What a strange plant to bring to someone in a hospital. But it's nice.

I tried to talk to the nun today, but she wouldn't answer. I asked her name, and if she works at the hospital, but she just smiled and put her finger to her lips. Then she put a book in my hands, heavy and leather bound. I assumed it would be a bible, but it's a book of the lives of the saints. I've always grown up with bibles around the house, but these stories are new to me. Our church doesn't talk about saints. The pastor says it's wrong to focus on anyone but Jesus. God. Whatever. I don't have anything else to read, though, since there's no Wi-Fi here.

It's full of illustrations, too, and some of them are pretty gory.

FRIDAY, MAY 30
(TRANSCRIBED FROM PENCIL AND PAPER)

I was reading those stories about these saints. A lot of them are very strange and seem not very realistic, like this story of Saint George, who saved a princess from a dragon, or Saint Ursula, who traveled all around Europe followed by eleven thousand virgins. That's hard to picture.

But then, most of the events happened a long time ago, and maybe some details got screwed up or exaggerated. Besides, if someone wrote a story of my life, I'm not sure how believable it would look, so maybe I shouldn't judge.

There's something strange about some of the stories, though. Something really familiar, which is weird, because I didn't grow up hearing these stories. It's not quite like I know the stories, but every once in a while there will be a word or an image that sticks out at me, and it's like a gong reverberating through my body, or something I've seen in a dream. Or déjà vu. But I can't quite put my finger on it.

FRIDAY, MAY 30 (LATER THE SAME DAY)
(TRANSCRIBED FROM PENCIL AND PAPER)

I just figured it out! I was reading about Saint Catherine and how she was tortured on a spiked wheel, and I remembered the spiked and flaming wheel I used to see when I had my attacks. And the picture of it that showed up on my blog. And I flipped through and found Saint Apollonia, who had all her teeth pulled out. And here's Saint Lawrence, who was roasted alive on a grill, and Saint Lucy, who had her eyes ripped out.

There are other stories I've run across where I see weirdly familiar pieces of my life pop up. Famous pilgrims carried seashells, and one lady escaped her tormenters by growing feathers and turning into a bird, and a few made roses grow where they normally wouldn't.

What does it all mean? It feels like puzzle pieces fitting together, but I can't see the whole picture yet. Oh, and some of the pictures show the saints holding palm branches like the one that nun brought for me. Is that important? Does it have something to do with being a saint? Is she trying to tell me she thinks I'm a saint? I can't be, though. I don't even believe in that stuff.

But I remember what Miss Pierre was telling me before I got taken away and shut up in here. About how sometimes a possession is from the Devil, but sometimes it's a message from God that you've been picked out for something special. But what? I always thought God's purpose for me was to sing, but I don't really think that anymore. At least, not in the way I was picturing.

SUNDAY, JUNE 1
(TRANSCRIBED FROM PENCIL AND PAPER)

Miss Pierre came to visit me today. Funny, since I was just thinking of her. It was nice to see her, and she said she had been very worried about me, and has prayed for me every day. I must look like hell, because as soon as she saw me, she got a shocked and pitying look on her face, and she stroked my cheek and muttered a prayer or some other protective spell, I'm not sure.

She said she could see I'd "endured a great torment at the hands of the spirits." No argument there. She grabbed my hands and begged me not to give in to despair. She said there had been so many signs. Signs that I had been chosen. And then she said, "I know there is doubt in your mind, but there is no doubt in mine. You have been chosen for greatness."

I know I always dreamed of that. Of being recognized as

special or "chosen." If this is what it means, though, I wish I had dreamed of something else. I understand now: there's a lot to be said for being ordinary.

Besides, it's a nice thing to say, but how can I trust it? And if I've really been chosen for something, when do I find out what it is? Is there something I should be doing now? I don't feel like I'm doing anything very special at the moment. Mostly just lying in bed and trying not to vomit or faint every time I sit up a bit. I don't really see how that's part of God's plan.

Miss Pierre said not to worry too much about it. That I should just trust in God, and it would all become clear. She makes it sound so simple! But how can it be? How can I trust any voice in my head or my heart when God and the Devil sound the same to me? But Miss Pierre did tell me long ago that the Devil works for God. Is that true? Maybe they speak with the same voice because there is no difference between them. I don't know whether that's comforting or terrifying.

Excerpt from telephone interview between
Professor M. Verano and Officer B████ of the
████████ County Police Department.

Date: 11/24/2014
Subject: Results of the investigation of the
██████████ residence for evidence of paranormal
activity.

VERANO: AND SHORTLY AFTER THE INCIDENT WITH L████, MS.
C████ J████ CONTACTED YOU, IS THAT RIGHT?

OFFICER B███: THAT'S CORRECT.

VERANO: AND WHAT DID SHE WANT?

OFFICER B████ SHE WANTED ME TO COME BACK TO THE
HOUSE. L████ WASN'T THERE ANYMORE, BUT HER MOTHER
HAD AN IDEA THAT THERE WAS SOME KIND OF . . .
[UNINTELLIGIBLE] ACTIVITY IN THE HOUSE. SHE WANTED
HELP LOOKING INTO IT. I GUESS SHE REMEMBERED HOW
SPOOKED I'D BEEN DURING THE PREVIOUS INCIDENT, AND SHE
THOUGHT I WOULD BE SYMPATHETIC TO HER MISSION.

VERANO: SO YOU AGREED TO RETURN TO MS. J████'S HOUSE?

OFFICER B████ YES, BUT OFF-DUTY. ON MY OWN TIME.

VERANO: WHY DID YOU AGREE TO IT?

OFFICER B███: I WAS CURIOUS, I GUESS. I COULDN'T STOP
THINKING ABOUT THAT GIRL. L████. I KNOW WHAT I SAW,
AND THAT WAS NOT NORMAL. THAT WAS NOT . . . IT WASN'T
ANYTHING THAT BELONGS IN THIS WORLD. AT THE TIME, WHEN

I SAW THAT, I JUST WANTED TO GET AS FAR AWAY FROM THAT HOUSE AND THAT FAMILY AS POSSIBLE. ACTUALLY, WHEN MS. J███ CALLED ME TO ASK IF I WOULD COME BACK, AT FIRST I HUNG UP ON HER. BUT THEN I STARTED TO GET CURIOUS. YOU DON'T BECOME A POLICE OFFICER UNLESS YOU LIKE MYSTERIES, YOU KNOW? I COULDN'T JUST WALK AWAY AND NOT GATHER ANY EVIDENCE.

VERANO: DO YOU BELIEVE IN THE SUPERNATURAL?

OFFICER B████: I DON'T KNOW. [UNINTELLIGIBLE] I BELIEVE IN GHOSTS, YEAH, BUT I NEVER THOUGHT THEY WERE HARMFUL. DEMONS? NO, I DON'T BELIEVE IN DEMONS. AT LEAST, I DIDN'T.

VERANO: SO YOU CONTACTED HER?

OFFICER B████: NO, I--I DIDN'T DO ANYTHING. BUT SHE CALLED AGAIN A COUPLE OF DAYS LATER, AND THIS TIME I HEARD HER OUT AND SAID I WOULD COME OVER TO HELP. I WAS STILL SCARED, BUT I WANTED TO KNOW. I'M NO COWARD.

VERANO: SO WHAT HAPPENED?

OFFICER B████: I WENT OVER ON A SUNDAY AFTERNOON. I WAS NERVOUS GOING IN, BUT THE HOUSE SEEMED PERFECTLY NORMAL THIS TIME. IT WAS DIFFERENT WITHOUT THE DAUGHTER THERE.

VERANO: CAN YOU DESCRIBE HOW IT WAS DIFFERENT?

OFFICER B████: DIFFERENT . . . ENERGY? I DON'T KNOW HOW TO DESCRIBE IT. LIKE THE DIFFERENCE BETWEEN GOING OUT ON A NICE SUNNY DAY VS. WALKING OUTSIDE AND

KNOWING A STORM IS COMING. SOMETHING IN THE LIGHT, IN THE AIR . . . DIFFERENT SMELL, MAYBE. ANYWAY, MS. J████ MADE ME A CUP OF COFFEE, AND WE DISCUSSED OUR APPROACH. SHE WAS CONVINCED THE NEGATIVE ENERGY WAS COMING FROM THE BASEMENT. I WENT DOWN THERE WITH A SHOVEL. . . . THE BASEMENT HAS A DIRT FLOOR. AND I SPENT AN HOUR OR TWO DIGGING, MOSTLY UNDER THE STAIRS WHERE SHE SAID THE [UNINTELLIGIBLE] WAS MOST POWERFUL. MS. J████ WAS CONVINCED SOMEONE LIVING IN THE HOUSE HAD PERFORMED SOME BLACK MAGIC RITUAL AND HAD OPENED A PORTAL THAT NEEDED TO BE CLOSED. SHE SAID IF I DUG UNDER THE STAIRS, WE WOULD FIND EVIDENCE. A OUIJA BOARD OR A MAGIC CIRCLE OR ANIMAL BONES, MAYBE.

VERANO: WHAT DID YOU FIND?

OFFICER B████: NOTHING, REALLY. JUST SOME RANDOM JUNK. A KID'S BRACELET, FAKE EYELASHES, A PAIR OF UNDERWEAR. I THOUGHT THAT MIGHT BE A CLUE TO SOME KIND OF TRAUMA OR ABUSE, BUT SINCE THE WASHER AND DRYER ARE DOWN THERE, THAT SEEMED LIKE A MORE LIKELY EXPLANATION. NOTHING THAT SEEMED MAGICAL OR CURSED OR ANYTHING.

OFFICER B████: AFTER THAT I TOOK A FEW MORE PICTURES AROUND THE HOUSE, IN PLACES WHERE MS. J████ THOUGHT SHE HAD DETECTED SPIRIT ACTIVITY. BUT IT ALL SEEMED PRETTY NORMAL.

VERANO: THERE WAS ONE PHOTO IN THE BATCH YOU SENT ME. . . . ONE LOOKING DOWN THE BASEMENT STAIRS.

OFFICER B████: YOU NOTICED THAT ONE, DID YOU? MOST PEOPLE LOOK AT IT AND DON'T NOTICE ANYTHING STRANGE ABOUT IT. I DIDN'T UNTIL MY DAUGHTER POINTED IT OUT TO ME.

VERANO: THERE'S A SHAPE THERE. LOOKS LIKE . . .

OFFICER B████: LOOKS LIKE SOMETHING, I KNOW. IT'S NOT A COAT RACK, THAT'S FOR SURE. BUT I CAN'T FIGURE OUT WHAT IT WAS. I MEAN, I CAN'T BE POSITIVE IT WASN'T JUST A WEIRD SHADOW, OR SOME GRIT ON THE LENS. SO.

VERANO: I SEE. YES. THANK YOU FOR YOUR TIME.

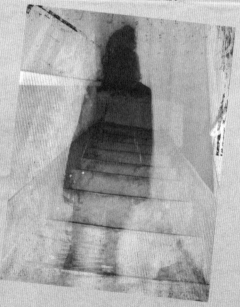

END EXCERPT

DEPARTMENT OF SOCIAL SERVICES
FAMILY RESOLUTION PLAN

Date: 6/2/2014   Family Surname: ███████████

PARENT/GUARDIAN INFORMATION

Father: Unknown, not involved   Mother: C██████

Other guardian: █████████, grandmother

Name of Child: L█████

Age: 15

GOAL: Reunification of family

CURRENT SITUATION:

L████ has been removed from C████'s household and placed in state custody in response to severe instability in the home. Previous to her removal, L███'s school attendance was inconsistent, and her home life was dominated by constant threats of "demonic interference." Social services caseworker R. S. determined the situation was encouraging violent, delusional, and antisocial tendencies in L█████. L███ is currently housed in a psychiatric facility. R. S. is working with C████ to improve the situation in the home, with the goal of L███'s eventual return. If C████ does not cooperate with the objectives, foster care is an alternative option for L█████.

BENEFITS OF REUNIFICATION:

C███ is a caring and attentive mother who has no history of physically or verbally abusive behaviors. C███ has a history of seeking help and accepting guidance when her family's situation is struggling or threatened. L███ is polite, well behaved, and sociable when not under the influence of her delusions. L███ and C███ have a strong mother-daughter bond, and both are motivated to do what is required to end their separation.

RISKS OF REUNIFICATION:

C███ is overly reliant on supernatural explanations for challenges faced by her family. L███ is suggestible to her mother's influence and prone to "playing along" to support her mother's delusions. Both have in the past struggled to comply with plans designed to improve their situation, and can be stubborn or secretive when pressed.

OBJECTIVES FOR PARENT/GUARDIAN/CUSTODIAL CARETAKER:

- Mother will ensure child attends school on a regular basis
- All absences and tardies will come with a justified excuse from someone outside the household
- Mother will participate in a clinical psychiatric assessment and comply with the recommendations

- Mother will seek explanations for events not directly related to religion or demonic infestation
- Mother and child will not use demonic possession as an excuse for child's behaviors

Signed:

██████████████████████████

Mother: ███████████
Caseworker: ███████████

I have my laptop back! Mamma brought it when she came to visit today. I guess that's the other big news: Mamma's probation period is over, and the social services people have declared her fit to have me in the house again! Which means I can go home as soon as the doctors here approve it.

I asked Mamma what changed their minds, and she said it was *her* mind, really, that got changed. She was so sure there was some demon infecting our house, but the more she tried to tell everyone about it, the more crazy and unstable they decided she was. Finally she decided she'd get some hard evidence no one could disagree with, and they'd all see this situation wasn't her fault. She had this idea that there was something in the basement, some kind of portal or something, that was allowing demons to come through and torment us. She got the cops to come over and search it with her, but I guess they didn't find anything much.

After that, she decided to let it go. She wanted me back, and it wasn't worth the fight anymore. So she told Renee and a judge and a counselor that she didn't believe in demons anymore, and that from now on she would look for earthly explanations for problems facing the household. She even signed something saying she wouldn't get in touch with Miss Pierre, and she wouldn't talk about demons with me anymore. (She made an exception today because she couldn't figure out how to explain to me what the agreement was without saying it.)

Then she explained I could come home and live with her and Gramma Patty as soon as I was feeling better. She asked me if I thought that might be soon, and I told her yes, I hoped so. She'd heard about my incident with the window and had been worried about me, but I told her about the nun who visited me, and how she had changed my whole outlook. How without even talking, she had made me feel more positive about my situation. I expected Mamma to be pleased about this, but she looked concerned instead. She touched my head as if feeling for a fever, even though I told her I was feeling better.

I asked her what the problem was and she said, "Baby, this isn't a Catholic hospital. And no one has come to see you here except Gramma Patty and Miss Pierre. I saw the logbook."

I guess that means she doesn't believe me that the nun visited me at all. That, just like the doctors, she thinks I'm imagining things or making them up.

I started to argue with her, but I gave up before long. I was too tired to pull together evidence that what I remembered really happened. And anyway, after all I've been through, how do I even know to trust myself? I've long since given up any sense of certainty about what I see and feel versus what other people do.

And then Mamma took my hand and was like, "Baby, can you do something for me? When the doctors come in and ask how you are feeling, just tell them you are feeling fine, all right? Your story about the nun, that can just be between us. "

I guess I see what she means.

DR.███: TELL ME ABOUT THE INCIDENT THAT PUT
YOU HERE, IN THE HOSPITAL. DO YOU REMEMBER
THAT?

L██: WHEN I ATTACKED THE POLICE OFFICERS?

DR. ██: YES.

L███ I REMEMBER.

DR███ AND WHAT ABOUT THE OTHER INCIDENT,
WHILE YOU WERE HERE?

L███ THE SUICIDE ATTEMPT.

DR.███ IS THAT WHAT IT WAS?

L███ PRETTY MUCH, YEAH. I THOUGHT IT WOULD
BE BETTER FOR EVERYONE IF I WASN'T ALIVE
ANYMORE. SO I DECIDED TO . . . YOU KNOW.
WHATEVER IT TOOK.

DR.███ AND HOW DO YOU FEEL ABOUT THAT NOW?

L███ I DON'T FEEL LIKE THAT, NOT ANYMORE. I
WAS ALL MIXED UP. NOW I JUST WANT TO SEE MY
MAMMA AND GRAMMA PATTY AGAIN. GET BACK TO
MY OLD ROOM, GO TO SCHOOL.

DR. ███ BUT YOU REMEMBER THOSE INCIDENTS.

L███ YEAH. YEAH, I REMEMBER THEM NOW.

DR. ███ YOU DIDN'T REMEMBER THEM BEFORE? THE
MEMORIES CAME BACK TO YOU AT SOME POINT?
I ███ NO, I ALWAYS KNEW WHAT HAPPENED. I
JUST . . . I DIDN'T WANT TO TALK ABOUT IT
BEFORE. I DIDN'T KNOW HOW TO TALK ABOUT IT.
DR. ███ CAN YOU EXPLAIN NOW WHAT YOU WERE
THINKING DURING THOSE INCIDENTS? WHAT
CAUSED THAT BEHAVIOR?
I ███ I BELIEVED I WAS POSSESSED BY A
POWERFUL DEMON THAT WAS TRYING TO DESTROY
ME AND MY FAMILY.
DR. ███ BUT THAT'S NOT WHAT YOU BELIEVE NOW?
I ███ NO. OR . . . I GUESS I'D SAY MY
PERSPECTIVE HAS CHANGED. I BELIEVE NOW
THAT MY FAMILY WAS DEALING WITH A LOT OF
PROBLEMS, AND I WAS DEALING WITH SOME
PROBLEMS. ANXIETY. DEPRESSION. TRYING TO
FIGURE OUT WHO I WAS, WHO I WANTED TO BE.
I WASN'T GOOD AT TALKING ABOUT IT. SO MAYBE
THE DEMONS I BELIEVED IN GAVE ME A WAY OF
TALKING ABOUT THAT STUFF.
DR. ███ WHAT DO YOU MEAN? DO YOU MEAN LIKE A
METAPHOR?
I ███ YEAH, THAT'S RIGHT. I THINK WE ALL HAVE
OUR DEMONS, BUT THE ONLY WAY TO GET RID OF
THEM IS . . . IT'S NOT MAGIC AND EXORCISMS.

YOU HAVE TO JUST FACE THE PROBLEMS YOU HAVE
HERE IN THIS WORLD.

AFTER REVIEWING THE PATIENT'S FILE, IT IS
CLEAR PATIENT #███████ HAS MADE REMARKABLE
PROGRESS WHILE UNDER OUR CARE. SHE NO
LONGER SUFFERS FROM THE DELUSIONS THAT
PLAGUED HER UPON ADMITTANCE. THERE
WAS SOME CONCERN THAT CONTACT WITH HER
MOTHER MIGHT CAUSE A REGRESSION, BUT
THIS DOES NOT APPEAR TO BE THE CASE. BOTH
MOTHER AND DAUGHTER HAVE AGREED TO FACE
THEIR PROBLEMS AND NOT BLAME THEM ON
SUPERNATURAL INTERFERENCE.
THE PATIENT'S MEDICAL TEAM HAS DECLARED
HER TREATMENT A SUCCESS AND CAN SEE NO
REASON FOR HER NOT TO BE RELEASED FROM
THE HOSPITAL. HER DISCHARGE IS APPROVED
IMMEDIATELY.

DISCHARGE DATE: 6/3/2014

THURSDAY, JUNE 5, 4:30 P.M. (PRIVATE)

It's nice to be home, but I'm having some trouble adjusting to normal life. I can't help feeling removed from it. There's school, and there are chores and meals and TV shows, but none of it feels like it has anything to do with me. The doctors say that's normal, and that it will get better with time, but I don't know. I feel almost like I'm just biding my time until . . . well, I don't know what. But like Miss Pierre said, I'll just listen carefully, and hopefully, it will become clear.

I set the palm the silent nun brought me on my window-sill. Mamma asked if I wanted to just leave it at the hospital or donate it to another patient. She doesn't think it's very nice looking, as plants go, and she did bring me a nice bright gera-nium, but it seemed important to hold on to the palm.

Maybe it's because of what Mamma said in the hospital—

that the nun wasn't real. If she was just my imagination, where did the plant come from? And the rosary, and the book of saints? Those feel real enough, and other people can see them. I've thought about asking Mamma if she could explain it, or maybe Miss Pierre, but maybe it doesn't need to be explained. Maybe I already know the answer.

SATURDAY, JUNE 21, 12:30 P.M. (PRIVATE)

I was looking at the local news, and I saw the *America Sings* auditions are here in town. I could hardly believe it, but when I looked at my calendar, I had marked it months ago. Funny to think how important that once was to me, and today I almost didn't even notice it was happening.

I sort of checked inside myself to see if there was any part of me that wished I were there today, but I don't think there is. The person I was then seems so far away now. I flipped back to my blog posts from before all this started, and I hardly recognize who I was then.

It's been a while since I've even updated here. Honestly, I'm not sure what to say. I spend so much of every day repeating the things I'm supposed to say, it feels weird to acknowledge the other things. The things I'm not supposed to talk about. But I guess there's no reason to hide them here.

I know Renee and the doctors will send me away if they get the sense I'm "acting out" again. And I don't want to leave. This is where I'm meant to be right now, with my family, so I'll keep my mouth shut. But the truth is, I've still got a lot of the old problems; I just know how to deal with them better now. I still have bad dreams and visions, and days when I can't tell one from the other. I still sometimes feel like my skin is on fire, or I get a horrible stabbing pain in my side, but instead of falling to the ground or crying out and drawing attention to myself, I just accept it. It's serving some purpose, though I don't know what yet. But I trust that.

Anyway, there are more important things to worry about. Like the protests that are still going on about the Robinson trial. The riots pretty much burned themselves out while I was in the hospital, but that doesn't mean people have forgotten about the injustice that was done. The crowd gathering at the park is bigger than ever, and now I'm with them too, the way I always should have been. Mamma and I, we haven't talked about it directly, but we have kind of an understanding now. She still worries about me going over there, but she understands it's important to me, I know the risks, and I have to make my own choices. So the deal is, I keep quiet about all the weird stuff that is still happening with me, and she doesn't object when I go to the park to help out with the protests.

When Miss Pierre told me to look inside myself for what I should be doing, it didn't take me long to figure out that I should be with the protesters. But I wasn't sure what I had to contribute, so I asked around and found out they needed people to bring water and sandwiches. At first that seemed kind of dull and insignificant compared to all the stuff I've been through recently, but they told me, "People have to eat!" And I guess that's true.

So I just started making sandwiches and going around the park with a basket of them, offering them to anyone who looked tired or hungry. I didn't really want to draw attention to myself. I was afraid that would seem prideful, as if I were only doing it so people would be impressed with me. At first I just went around, my head wrapped in a scarf and not saying more than, "Hi, are you hungry?" to anyone. But then the other day an old teacher I had freshman year recognized me and said she remembered how I always used to have brightly colored hair. She said whenever she saw it, it was like a bit of sunshine in her day. Then she said people there in the park could use a little of that sunshine.

At first I felt awkward about it. The flashy hair was who I used to be, when all I cared about was being famous and singing in huge arenas and getting a lot of hits on my blog. It didn't feel appropriate to the serious work of protesting racial injustice. But the more I thought about it, the more I realized I missed it. My colorful wigs are part of who I am. What's the shame in that? And if they bring other people a little happiness and good cheer, maybe that's not such a bad thing. Maybe it could help raise morale.

So now I'm thinking I'll try it out. I've already played around with styling my turquoise wig tonight. We'll see what kind of reaction I get when I wear it tomorrow.

SUNDAY, JUNE 22, 5:32 P.M. (PRIVATE)

I showed up today at the protests in the turquoise wig with glittery pink barrettes. Other than that, I was just doing my normal stuff, walking around the park with my basketful of sandwiches. But it was weird—I felt totally different. I've gradually been feeling better about things ever since the old nun came to me, but this was the first time I could remember in ages where I really felt . . . glad to be me. To be alive. Confident and happy.

I think other people noticed it too, unless they were just responding to the wig. A few of them did mention they were happy to see me smiling. I guess I had looked pretty serious before. It was also useful, because people can spot me from far away. So if people need water or medical attention, they can tell someone to look for the girl with bright hair, and I'll come and help them. Now I'm not just handing out a few sandwiches. I can help a lot more people.

TUESDAY, JUNE 24, 6:53 P.M. (PRIVATE)

Guess who I ran into at the park today! Angela! I guess she's been coming to the protests for a couple of weeks, but she spotted me today because of the wig.

It was so good to see her again. We left things on kind of bad terms, but somehow it was easy to forget about all that today. She gave me a big hug and asked how I was doing. I thought about telling her all the stuff I've been through—the trances and the hospitalization and everything—but why drag up all that stuff? It doesn't really matter anymore. It seemed better to just talk about the Robinson trial and the demonstrations, and the work we're all doing together. She's excited about it too.

It's nice to have something in common again. Instead of fighting about whether to talk about my life or hers, we can talk together about something we both care about.

While I was catching up with her, one of Mamma's old friends from church came up to say hi. She told me she'd seen me around the park, but she didn't recognize me until I started wearing my wigs again. Then she asked me why I don't sing anymore.

I told her about how I used to sing, but one day I lost my voice. I kind of left it at that, figuring she didn't need to know all the other crap. Anyway, she just brushed it off and said it didn't matter. Singing is fun, and it doesn't matter if your voice is perfect or you sound like a professional. Funny, it's been ages since I thought of it that way. When I was a little girl and Mamma was teaching me songs, I loved to sing just for the joy of it. Then I started to get noticed, and it turned into a whole thing, with ambitions and pressures to succeed. . . . I still loved it, but in a different way.

I explained to her that it didn't matter—it's not just that my voice is no good; it's gone completely. But the woman hardly paid attention. She just started singing some old protest song, and Angela joined in, and so did a bunch of other people. And I sort of half knew the words from hearing other people sing it these past few weeks, and they all were having so much fun that I desperately wanted to join in. It's the first time I've really missed singing in ages and ages. So I just started mouthing the words so I wouldn't feel so left out. And then I was singing really softly under my breath . . . and then I tried it a little louder . . . and what do you know? I was singing again! It's true, my voice isn't as big and polished as it used to be, but it didn't seem to matter, because everyone around me was singing along and joining in, and no one was trying to be a soloist or be the best. We were all just having a good time and lifting one another's spirits.

That in itself would have been enough to make this a pretty amazing day, but then something else happened. I got all lit up with this sudden fire to write a song of my own. I don't know where it even came from! I've never been able to write songs before, not even a little. But as I was walking home that evening, I could hear the whole thing in my head—the tune and the words and everything. I was so excited, I actually started running the last few blocks, so I could write it all down before I forgot it. And once I sat down, I couldn't stop. Song after song just poured right out of me. I think I have six or seven written up now!

They're all just about joining together with other people for a cause. They're supposed to cheer people up, and maybe help our message spread wider. I hope people like them. I can't wait to go back to the park tomorrow and share them.

WEDNESDAY, JUNE 25, 9:42 P.M. (PRIVATE)

Today was amazing! I use to think singing was the greatest feeling in the world, but I had no idea what it would feel like to hear other people singing songs I made up. And best of all, it's supporting a cause that's really important. Finally I feel useful to the world. And everyone—Gramma, Renee, my friends at the park—they all say such a change has come over me in the past few weeks.

Though the truth is, a lot of that is just how I present myself. I've learned how to share the good stuff and hide the stuff that's, well . . . it's not bad, but it's harder for a lot of people to understand.

That reminds me: I finally figured something out about that plant the nun gave me.

I was curious, so I looked up palms online. Now I know why some of the saints are carrying palms and some aren't: the palm is a symbol of martyrdom. It marks out the saints who died for their beliefs.

I'm not sure how I feel about that. Was the nun trying to tell me that will happen to me? I don't want that, but the surprising thing is, I'm not as scared of it as I used to be. As I feel like I should be. Like most people, dying used to seem like the scariest thing in the world. Partly because I didn't know what it would be like, and partly because I was afraid I wouldn't get a chance to achieve my goals and dreams.

When I first read what the palm meant, I had this moment of . . . I don't know. It's like I paused a minute and looked inside myself, expecting to feel that jolt of terror most normal humans get when they picture their own deaths. But it never came. I just felt calm, and like I was finally understanding something I'd half known all along. Now I don't feel like death is a mystery. In the past few months, I've spent so much time and energy dealing with the spiritual world, it doesn't seem as foreign to me as it used to. And I feel pretty confident there is more than emptiness and nonexistence on the other side.

As for achieving my dreams, my dreams aren't what they once were. My new dreams are what I'm doing right now. All my life I was so sure I was special and I'd been marked for some kind of greater purpose. Now it seems crazy I ever thought I was fated to be a pop star when there are things in this world so much bigger and more important than celebrating my own glory.

Was the nun sent to tell me I'm going to die for this cause?

That I'll be martyred like the other people in that book? I don't want to die, especially not now, when I feel almost like I've just come back to the world of the living, but at least I know what I'm here for now, and this doesn't change that.

Editor's Note
2/7/2015

The writer known in these pages as Laetitia did continue to volunteer at the protests in [redacted] Park. Though she apparently lost interest in updating her journal, she rapidly became known for the protest songs she would sing as she offered people food and water. During the next few weeks, she was struck by a rare creative energy and seemed to compose almost in a frenzy. Those close to her say she was more joyful and determined in this period than during any other time in her life.

Tragically, on July 2, 2014, there was an altercation between the protesters and the police at the park that turned violent and ultimately deadly. Details are still unclear and will perhaps never be known with any great certainty, but according to witnesses, a mentally unstable man who was not well known at the protests and had only participated occasionally was the root of some disturbance. Members of the police force allegedly fired their weapons at him, and a stray bullet struck Laetitia in her side. She died in a hospital downtown later that day.

According to her mother, the site of the entry wound was exactly the spot that had so frequently and mysteriously pained Laetitia in the preceding months.

Since the incident, the songs Laetitia wrote have become popular not just within her city but at peaceful gatherings around the country.

Though the lasting accomplishments of this author and the tragic injustice of her death are beyond dispute, it's not for me to say whether the forces that afflicted her in her last few months were demonic or divine. No doubt there are those skeptical few who will refuse either suggestion, and claim that all the described events can be explained as medical or psychological anomalies.

If I may make any request of those who read the preceding document, it is to put aside such disingenuous skepticism, and consider how such solitary suffering might be avoided in the future. Both science and compassion command us to recognize that Laetitia's ordeal had as real a cause as any condition described by the medical establishment. It is only through serious academic inquiry into such long-ignored phenomena that we may one day offer hope to the similarly afflicted.

Montague Verano, Phd
Professor, Department of History
University of Idaho